Two Sieges of the Alamo

Francis "Tack" Tackett was a cub pilot on a Mississippi stern-wheeler. When he aids a runaway slave, he also becomes a fugitive. Tack then finds himself and three others setting out to join the Texas revolt. After a perilous journey to San Antonio de Bexar, the four join the polyglot Texan army that is besieging the town. Shortly after, Tack takes part in the first siege of the Alamo.

On March 6, 1836, the Alamo was taken in the second siege by the Mexican general Santa Anna. Robert Edmond Alter dramatically and accurately writes of this famous battle in American history, a battle where brave men without hope of victory knew it was a "time to stand."

TWO SIEGES of the ALAMO

BY ROBERT EDMOND ALTER

ILLUSTRATED BY ALBERT ORBAAN

G. P. PUTNAM'S SONS   NEW YORK

To Walter Lord, for his inspirational and informative book
A Time to Stand

I'll weave the chord and twine in,
Man's desire and babe's desire, I'll twine them in, I'll put in life,
I'll put the bayonet's flashing point, I'll let bullets and slugs whizz,
(As one carrying a symbol and menace far into the future,
Crying with trumpet voice, *Arouse and beware! Beware and arouse!*)
I'll pour the verse with streams of blood, full of volition, full of joy,
Then loosen, launch forth, to go and compete,
With the banner and pennant a-flapping.

—WALT WHITMAN,
"Song of the Banner at Daybreak"

Courageous men fight best when they have no illusions.

—WILLIAM BARRET TRAVIS
1809–1836

PROLOGUE

Dawn was established. The rolling badlands stretched away in it and became lost in the retreating darkness. The new light picked up the scrubby mesquite trees and an occasional live oak and a great sea of waving grass and wild flowers. The mesa turned lumpy, humping into mounds and eroded systems of steep little hills cut separate by white scars of sand, where the spring water had flowed. Then the true hills began.

And all of it was uninhabited. Hundreds of thousands of empty acres.

This great slab of land was Spain's cushion of space, acting as a buffer between her mines in Mexico and the land-hungry Americans in the north. They called this space Texas, and they saw no reason why its status quo should ever change.

Then the Indians came, the Comanches, with 5,000

braves, and they decided with a grunted *ugh* that Texas was theirs.

The Spanish authorities went into a tizzy. They were afraid they might lose Texas to the marauders. What to do? In desperation they turned to the American pioneers. They made a deal.

So in 1821 they offered a land grant to a man called Moses Austin, giving him permission for an American colony in Texas. But Moses up and died, leaving the concession to his son Stephen. And in that same year Mexico declared its independence from Spain.

Austin formed a contract with the new Mexican Republic —the Colonization Law of 1824. It was pretty good; it invited foreigners to settle in Texas for ten years free of taxes and duties. It gave every pioneer 4,428 acres for thirty dollars. It gave a guarantee of self-government under the Mexican Constitution of 1824.

The honeymoon was on between Mexico and the United States.

It was like the bursting of a dike. It exploded over the empty land, disgorging a living wash of hungry-eyed, expectant, impatient, bearded men and bonneted women. They came with their long rifles and axes, their Bibles and little bags of seed corn. They cleared, built, planted, reaped, stayed.

And they kept coming . . . and coming . . . and coming . . .

All at once the Mexican government sat up and opened its eyes and had a good look around.

"*Nombre de perro, amigos!* What is happening here?"

What was happening indeed! It was only 1830 and already the Americans controlled 75 percent of the Texas population. 30,000 American pioneers in only six years!

Vaminos with the Constitution of 1824! the Mexican government decided. No more settlers; no more colonists' coastal shipping; no more duty exemption for pioneers; Mexican troops to be stationed all over Texas; martial law to be strictly enforced and lock up any big-mouthed American who objected.

The honeymoon was over.

Austin objected mildly and was thrown into a Mexico City jail. A young firebrand called William Barret Travis objected violently and was thrown into the Anáhuac jail. And for a suspenseful moment it looked as if Texas might loggerhead itself into war.

But just then the Texans stopped short and said: Wait a minute, there's another revolution going on in Mexico. Let's hold on and see what they're going to do down there first. Let's see what this new president of theirs is like.

They weren't long in finding out. A bloody-minded anti-American general seized control of the Mexican government and set himself up as a dictator. His name was General Antonio López de Santa Anna.

A spoke in the wheel of history had started its crazy, significant spin.

I

WHAT YOU'RE DOING IS AGAINST THE LAW, YOU KNOW

From the rectangular glass pilothouse standing templelike on the texas, Tack felt like a god as he looked down on the *Anthony Wayne*'s foredeck and out along the great Mississippi. Adeptly, he put the man-tall wheel over a spoke to skirt some snaggle-toothed cypress stumps sticking out of the shallows, and then brought her back into the slack water along the swampy shore.

The first lesson he had learned as a cub pilot was to stick in the current going downriver, and to hug the easy water inside when going upriver. Old Ben Burrows, the regular pilot, held to this edict even if it meant that the *Anthony Wayne* had to shave off the paddle guards of half the stern-wheelers laying along the levee.

Tack glanced over his shoulder at the pilot's sofa—a showy red-leather affair, which through the years had more or less adopted itself to the contours of Ben Burrows' angular frame.

Ben was sprawled on his spine, working the chaw in his

9

lantern jaw with absentminded enjoyment, reading the August number of the *Ladies' Repository*. He was following a serial in the magazine which concerned a young girl called Fanny Preston, who had more adverse luck than you could shake a stick at.

"What's gone and happened to Fanny this month?" Tack asked. He really didn't much care about Fanny and her problems, which always seemed somewhat contrived and improbable to him, but he knew Ben got a kick out of recounting Fanny's misadventures.

Ben aimed a brown spit at the tarnished cuspidor in the corner and made a wet bull's-eye.

"Almighty big doin's, Tack! You recall that fella Fanny went to save in the snowstorm last month? Well, turns out he's one a them air Erie Canal highwaymen! Yessir. And now the townsfolk is all a-ganging up on Fanny's house fixin' to hang him, and Fanny don't know what to do about hit and all in a dither 'cause she cain't find her pa's rifle-gun to hold off the lynch mob with."

"Why doesn't she just take the highwayman's pistol?" Tack said.

Ben shifted his chaw from right cheek to left peevishly.

"Well—well, mebby she don't know he *got* one!"

"Well, she ought. You 'n' I know it. It fell right out of his coat when she dragged him into the house in last month's installment, didn't it? What's she got for a brain anyhow, a mud hive?"

Ben clawed at his chin whiskers furiously. Then he looked up with a gleam of triumph in his fierce eye.

"Well, but that was *a whole month ago*! You just said so yourself, Tacky. How kin you expect a pore rattled gal to remember a little detail like that for a whole month!"

"Rattled is right," Tack muttered. He looked forward again. A tall square gleaming-white steamboat was coming down on them, her great double stacks belching a glory of smoke into the sky.

"*General Gates* coming down," Tack said, and he reached for the whistle cord. The *Wayne* went *whoomp whoomp* in salutation.

Old Ben near to leaped right out of his sofa.

"Tack! Give a man a word a warning, cain't you? Near to made me swallow my chaw cuttin' loose like that!"

Tack grinned. "Your trick, Ben. I owe me some breakfast."

Ben set aside his magazine and got up grumbling in his whiskers.

"Don't know why I ever picked you off the levee and brung you in my pilothouse. Give me nothin' but lippityness all the time!"

"Same reason you trained Joss Peters two years ago," Tack told him. "So you could lazy around on that sofa and read how Fanny forgot about a pistol she tripped over four times, while some cub does all your work for you."

"Hit ain't so she tripped over it four times!" Ben yelled, as Tack started down the ladder to the hurricane deck. " '*Twas only oncet!* And you blame well know hit!"

Tack stopped at the bulletin board on the port texas wall to see if they'd picked up any interesting notices in New Orleans. There wasn't much new; the trouble in Texas still seemed to be progressing with a dogged determination that would probably lead to rebellion. . . .

An article from the *New Orleans Bee* dated October 12, 1835, said the Mexicans had tried to take a cannon from 160 Texans at Gonzales . . . the Texans had taunted the soldiers by defying them to "Come and take it" . . . someone had fired, the cannon had roared, the Mexicans had fled. . . . A Captain Collinsworth had captured Goliad. . . . Santa Anna's brother-in-law, General Martin Perfecto de Cós, was holding the key Texas town of San Antonio de Bexar with 400 troops. . . .

Another article from the *Red River Herald* urged all Americans to "come forward and assist your brethren" in

11

Texas' fight for liberty; and an ex-governor of Tennessee, a man called Sam Houston, who was now a big wheel in Texas politics, had written: "Let each man come with a good rifle and 100 rounds of ammunition—and come soon!"

Huh! So they really meant to go through with it after all. The Texans were going to fight for their independence. Nor were they going to do it alone; men were coming from every state in the Union to answer the appeal for help. Some of them were on board the *Wayne* right now. And Tack had seen a gang of slaves sweating to load cannons and powder kegs aboard the schooner *Columbus* at New Orleans. The shipment had been slated for Texas.

And a Cajun he knew had told him that he had passed plenty of abandoned backwoods shanties with G.T.T. (Gone To Texas) scrawled on their cabin doors.

Tack shrugged and turned away. The squabble in Texas wasn't his concern. He had no stake in that vast sprawling raw country. Anyhow, he'd rather be a steamboat pilot than a soldier any day. Tack liked adventure as much as the next eighteen-year-old; but he wasn't in favor of seeking a form of adventure that too often demanded your life or limb—namely war.

A young man in a beaver hat and a natty gray suit was standing on the stern of the hurricane deck. He appeared to be readjusting the tarp over the covered lifeboat. Seemingly satisfied with his work, he glanced quickly around—not spotting Tack—and vanished.

Tack waited a minute, then slipped back to the deserted stern deck. The boat was up on chocks and he had to rise on tiptoes to get his chin up to the gunwale. He lifted the edge of the tarp to peer inside the warm, shadowy confines of the boat.

Two things happened in the same instant: a brown hand shot behind his head and got a death grip on the back of his neck, and the dull glint of a knife blade flashed in his face.

For a moment Tack stared cross-eyed at the mean-looking blade held right under his nose. Then he swallowed and got his wits working again and looked into a pair of white-marbled eyes.

"Boy," the Negro with the knife in the boat said, "you go to open your mouth jes a speck an' I got to slice you."

Tack nodded agreeably—which took some doing, what with his chin on the gunwale and the weighty tarp on his head and the Negro's iron-fingered grasp on the back of his neck. But he managed it.

So what to do next? They couldn't stay that way indefinitely.

"What I gwine do wif you now?" the Negro asked worriedly.

Tack decided to risk opening his mouth a speck.

"I dunno. If you let go of me I might think of something."

"Uh-*uh*! Man, I ain't *about* to leggo you!"

"Well, how about me getting in there with you and we'll talk it over?"

13

The Negro wet his lips, his eyes sideslipping distractedly.

"You cain't climb up here with ma han' on your neckbone. An' if I leggo, you bound to run off an' tell on me."

"Suppose I give my word not to run and tell?" Tack offered.

"But can we trust your word?" A voice spoke at his back.

Tack tried to twist his head to see who was behind him, but the Negro set the point of the knife under his right eye, holding him.

"Who's dat?" he whispered frantically.

"How in blazes can I tell?" Tack hissed, half-strangled. "Get that blame thing out of my eye, will you?"

"All right, Joe. Let him go," the voice behind Tack spoke again. "It's all right. It's me—Henry Warnell."

The pressure on Tack's neck relaxed and he came down on his boot soles and turned. The young man in the beaver hat was standing beside him. Tack looked him over quickly and decided that he could take Warnell in a fair fight. Yet there was something about the pale spare-built youth that gave the impression of a steel hardness not wholly physical: an inner determination of purpose—which probably meant that Hank Warnell would be hard to handle.

"Fugitive slave, huh?" Tack nodded toward the lifeboat.

"Yes," Hank Warnell admitted. "He ran away from a breaking camp. I met him along the Lake Pontchartrain road. A slave chaser had been after him for a week and Joe was all done in. Half-starved among other things. He appealed to me for help and I—well, I couldn't simply turn my back on him, could I?"

A breaking camp. Tack knew of them. They were special camps for rily new slaves from the Congo, or for any plantation slave who had turned mean. They did to a man just what the name implied—they broke him in spirit, made him as docile as a pet rabbit.

"No," he said, "I guess you couldn't. Listen, we'd all better get into that boat and have a talk, before someone spots us. What you're doing is against the law, you know."

"The same applies for you—if you get into that boat with us."

"Get in," Tack said.

They hunkered around each other in a triangle under the tarp.

"I jes couldn't stick that ol' camp one more day," Joe told Tack in a whisper. "I hit one guard an' took off. You know what dey do to me if dey kotch me again."

Yes, Tack knew, but he didn't like to think about it. This was the first time in his life that slavery had become a personal issue with him. Now he suddenly found that he was being forced into taking sides, like it or not.

Still, the situation had an aspect of adventure about it that appealed to his nature. After all, nobody would stand him against a wall and shoot him if he elected to help a runaway slave. So—

"What's your plan?" he asked Hank Warnell.

"Joe says he's heard of an abolitionist in Baton Rouge who will endeavor to run any fugitive slave up north. So, my only plan at the moment is to get Joe to Baton Rouge."

"Did you make a clean getaway out of New Orleans?"

"No," Hank admitted. "That's the rub. This man Toff Beeker, the slave chaser, was only one jump behind us. I've got an idea he knows that Joe is on this boat."

Tack knew Toff Beeker—a big rough keg of a man, surly as a bear but shrewd in the ways of his dubious profession.

"Not so good," he said. "Beeker's bound to be waiting for this boat in Dillsburg."

Hank nodded. "That's why I hid Joe in this lifeboat."

"You might as well have tried to hide him standing up on top of the pilothouse," Tack said. "You think Beeker's a fool? Nearly every stowaway tries to get into a lifeboat. Beeker knows that. One of the first places he'll look."

15

"What'll we do then?" Hank asked.

"Suppose you wanted to hide a leaf. Where would you put it?"

"Uh—in a forest, I suppose. Among all the other leaves."

Tack grinned. "And if you wanted to hide a colored man?"

"I go you!" Hank cried. "Among the firemen."

"You've got it," Tack said. "Now—do you have any money?"

"Not very much," Hank said with a stiffening in voice and manner. "About twenty dollars. It's all I have between me and Texas."

"It's not for *me*," Tack snapped. "It's for the engineer. He'll do anything for money, but he won't wink his eye without it. Let me have ten of it."

"I'm sorry that I misunderstood your intentions," Hank said lamely. "I really didn't mean to insult—"

"Forget it. Meet me in the saloon in about fifteen minutes. C'mon, Joe. You're going to work."

Chief Engineer Amos Rynd was a little man, little in body, mentality and spirit. He gave Tack a surly hangdog look, not bothering to even glance at the Negro Joe tagging meekly along.

"You know what that old fromp of a skipper jest tolt me, Tack?" Amos cried above the backblast of the furnaces and the unholy row of the toiling deckhands and firemen and roustabouts. "Tolt me he'd kick me spang over the stern if I messed up his pretty decks jest once more with my cindery boots! *Me!* Said that to me, he did. Right in front a the crew! The turnip-toed, potato-nosed old sot!"

Tack shook his head sympathetically. He wanted Amos on his side right at the moment. Thing was, he knew that Captain Pennypacker meant it when he vowed he'd kick Amos off the boat; good riddance, too—at any other time but now.

16

"I've got something here that'll perk you up." Tack let Amos have a glimpse of the ten-dollar bill. Amos came to abrupt attention, like a hunting dog picking up fox scent.

"What's that you got thar, Tacky? Something fer me, eh?"

"Could be. If you have something for me."

"Like what?" Amos glanced suspiciously at Joe.

"Like making room in your black gang for one more fireman."

"Namely him?" Amos nodded at Joe.

"That's it."

"The ten dollar goes with him?"

"He's wearing it like a price tag, Amos."

Amos' ferretlike eyes took on a degree of craftiness.

"I don't hold with helpin' fugitive slaves, Tacky," he said in a low voice. "Hit's agin my principles."

Tack nodded, tucking the bill back into his pocket.

"I go you. It's against my principles to force money on a man that doesn't have use or need for it."

"Wait! Now don't go to git so all-fired rily, Tack. I didn't say I wouldn't *listen to reason*, now did I? Now did I, Tacky? What I started to say was ten dollars ain't a hull lot fer a man to break the Fugitive-Slave Law over. That's all I started to say."

"I see," Tack said, taking out the bill again and snapping it in and out accordion-like under Amos' avaricious eyes. "Well, it's a pity this here ten is all the money I have— seeing that it's not enough for a man of your principles to put this Negro to work in your gang and to keep your mouth shut about him if some man comes around asking for him."

The ten-dollar bill went *snap-snap* in his hands.

"What I mean to say," Tack continued, "is that you wouldn't have *to know* that you were breaking any law, because nobody that I know of has mentioned to you that this man is a fugitive. Yeah—it seems to me that as far as

17

you know he's just another fireman. But—like you say—you have principles . . ."

Amos' clawed hand shot out and snapped up the bill before Tack could restore it to his pocket.

"Boy," Amos snarled at Joe, "you git over thar and jine that gang feedin' pine knots to the furnaces!" He followed Tack over to the companionway, saying wheedlingly, "Thing is, Tacky, a ten-dollar bill ain't a hull lot fer the risk involved, is what."

It was imperative at this stage of the game that Tack kept Amos on his side. He looked back with a conspirator smile.

"Tell you, Amos. You look me up on payday. I'm a reasonable man. Maybe if we look hard enough we'll find a mate to that ten-dollar bill I just lost track of somewhere down here."

Amos chuckled. "Mebby we will, Tacky. Mebby we will."

Tack went up to the boiler (second) deck. He had a bad taste in his mouth from dealing with Amos Rynd. It seemed to him that no matter how pure a man's motives might be in the beginning of any enterprise, sooner or later he had to get down in the mud with the pigs and barter—if he hoped to obtain his ultimate goal.

Well, he thought his favorite thought, *it doesn't really matter, does it?* He went into the saloon.

The *Anthony Wayne*'s saloon might have been lifted out of a page of *Ivanhoe*; it was that baronial, that ornate. It was like looking down a long gaudy tunnel, resplendent with red-plush chairs and booths, with snow-white linen and sparkling decanters and silverware and crystal chandeliers. The magenta carpet was a miracle in thickness and softness, like walking on a colored cloud. All the windows sparkled, all the brass gleamed, all sound was muted and refined, modified according to the needs of civilized relaxation.

Hank Warnell was sitting in a booth with two dapper-looking, olive-skinned gentlemen. One of the gentlemen had a deck of playing cards in his slender, capable hands.

"*Que pasa, compadres?*" Tack said to them, smiling.

The dapper gentlemen glanced up at him with eyes as sharp and bright as bayonet points. Then the older of the pair spoke.

"Merely a friendly game, Tack."

"*No con mi amigo,*" Tack said. Not with my friend.

The Spanish gentlemen hesitated a moment, then smiled and shrugged. "*Por favor, amigo,*" the older one said. They got up and left. Tack slid into a seat.

"Riverboat gamblers," he explained. "They'd strip you bare."

Hank studied him with interest. "You speak Spanish, eh?"

"*Si, compadre*. And French. I was raised in New Orleans. It's a continental city."

"What are you doing on a riverboat?" Hank wondered.

Tack shrugged. "Ran away from home because my dad wanted me to go into banking with him. Not much fun in that, is there?"

"Perhaps you should go with me. After we take care of Joe."

"You mean to Texas? I remember you mentioned it earlier."

"Yes," Hank said. "I'm from Boston, and as soon as I read in the *Morning Post* of what was happening in Texas I caught the first ship out. Unfortunately, it was only going as far as Mobile. I've been on the road ever since. Two weeks now."

"Going to fight for liberty, eh?" Tack said.

"That's right. But why smile about it? Has the word so lost its shine since the Revolutionary War that it's become a joke?"

No, the word had not yet lost its glow from overuse. It was still the most important word in America. Americans,

19

in 1835, would still rather think of Liberty than of Security, Money, Power. It was a word with depth. It had substance. It was an American word.

"Sorry," Tack said. "I didn't mean to mock you or the Texans. But as far as I can see this fight is a dispute outside of our country. It doesn't concern you and me. It doesn't really matter, does it?"

"Yes, it does," Hank said.

"Why?"

"Because Americans are involved in it. Because I believe that if *one* American has to fight anywhere in the world for his rights, then *all* Americans are tradition-bound to help him."

Tack signaled to the saloon tender to bring him his breakfast. Warnell was stretching the limits of patriotism, from Tack's point of view. But there was no reason to start an argument about that; because patriotism was a subject with many tributaries of thought. Instead he merely voiced his opinion concerning war in general.

"Tell you, Hank. I get enough excitement right here along the Mississippi. The thing I have against war is, men get killed—a whole heap of men."

"That's right," Hank said. "Men were killed at Gonzales and Goliad. Americans, like you and me. More will be killed at San Antonio de Béxar before this is over. But for a very valid reason. Whether you know it or not—without Texas, this country of ours is like a bull with only three legs, geographically speaking."

Tack tried to picture the enormous, ungainly spread of the United States, geographically. But it was too much of a mental chore. His mind was already too full of the names of the towns, points, bars, islands, bends, reaches, elbows, and horseshoes of the Mississippi: all the necessary landmarks and watermarks that a cub pilot had to have down pat. He grinned at Hank.

"Well, I wish you and the Texans luck with your fourth

20

leg of the Union. But I've got my hands geographically full of this river."

Hank looked at him soberly.

"I honestly wish you would come with me. I think you'd be good for Texas."

"Me?" Tack said. "Shucks, what would one more man mean to Texas? Sorry, Hank, but I know when I'm well off. Anyhow," he said, turning to the white-jacketed waiter who approached with a platter of ham and eggs and pone, "it doesn't really matter, does it?"

2

YOU GIVE THEM MEXICANS
HECK FOR ME

The *Anthony Wayne* rounded a horseshoe turn just above Dillsburg. Looking out from the pilothouse, Tack saw the little point of town with its one wharf and its small collection of stores, church, and homes; the daily idlers loafing back in the splint-bottom chairs along the porches, the stray dog or pig rooting under the exposed mud around the piles, the town sot dozing complacently on top of the levee.

What's wrong with them? Tack wondered. All of those idle old men and bums. Are they real? Are they actually a living part of this country, that they can spend their whole lives lazying around on porches spitting and whittling and telling each other lies about the Revolutionary War and the War of 1812?

Then he thought about himself. Was he any better than they were? *Men were killed at Gonzales and Goliad. Americans, like you and me,* Hank had said. And what did he do about it? Nothing. He simply continued to go up and down the old river, as complacent in his own way as the town sot sleeping in the shade of the levee.

Angrily he reached for the cord and the bronchial whistle screamed up the river. Instantly a Negro drayman cut loose with the classic cry:

"S-t-e-a-mboat a-comin'! Steamboat round the b-e-nd!"

The town came to life like a heated ant nest, with kids and women and Negroes and aproned shopkeepers popping up all over the place, all trotting down to the main stem of the little river town, the wharf. Even the sot managed to show a little interest, though he showed it in the wrong style. He forgot he was on the levee and he took a wrong turn when he staggered to his feet and he fell into the river; which gave everyone a good haw-haw and gave the sot a much-needed bath.

Captain Pennypacker, standing on the hurricane, clanged his bell proudly, and Ben whooped down the speaking tube for Stop Wheels and then Full Astern, and the paddle box started back-churning a glory of foam as the gauge cocks began whistling and moaning out their pent-up steam, and a deckhand went out on the broad stage over the port bow with a coiled rope in his hands.

Tack spotted Toff Beeker standing on the wharf.

"Back in a minute, Ben. Got to see somebody."

"Hey!" Ben yelled after him. "You just got here, blame it!"

Tack wasn't in any hurry when he reached the boiler deck. He put his hands in his pockets and sauntered along like a man killing time. He pretended not to notice Toff Beeker at first.

"Tack! Hey, Tackett, wait a minute. I want a word with you."

Tack looked around and said, "Oh. Hi, Toff. Going upriver?"

Beeker came at Tack as if he meant to bowl him over. He always walked that way, leading with his head. His eyes

23

were small and mean, stupidly mean; they wore the kind of look you expected to find behind a knife in a dark alley.

"Tack, any strange colored men get aboard in New Orleans?"

"Why?" Tack asked innocently. "You lose a friend?"

"Don't smart off at me, boy. You know dang well why! I'm after a fugitive slave."

"That so? What's he look like?"

"Big surly fella. Has some bluish lash scars on his back. He was wearin' a tattered old pink work shirt when I seen him last."

Tack spat over the rail, taking his own sweet time. He was enjoying this. "Does he know how to swim?"

Beeker looked impatiently bewildered. "*Swim?* How do I know kin he swim er not! What you gittin' at, anyhow?"

"Oh, just wondering."

"You playing with me, Tack? You keeping something from me?"

Tack leaned against the rail negligently. "Maybe," he said.

Beeker took Tack's arm in his thick hand.

"I put a lot a time and some a my own money in this business, boy. I cain't afford to let this fugitive git away. I got reason to believe they's a white man helpin' this slave. And I got reason to believe they boarded this boat in New Orleans. Now you want me to go git the high sheriff and keep this boat tied up here at Dillsburg for hours while we go through it piece by piece?"

Tack grinned at the angry man. "You've told me all about this fugitive except for the interesting part—the reward price."

A hint of speculation gleamed in Beeker's eyes.

"Ah, you *do* know something, huh? All right. It's two hunnert dollars. That's what I git, less my time 'n' expenses, if I catch him. Now—if you help me—I *might* give you five percent."

24

Tack rubbed at his right ear. "How's that again?"

"Jehoshaphat! All right, all right. Ten percent."

"Half down to bind the bargain," Tack said. "The other half when you catch him."

Beeker cursed profanely under his breath—but dug up the money.

"All righty, where's he hidin' on this scow?"

"He's not," Tack said. "But I know where he *was* hiding."

"Boy, are you trying to fleece me? Because if you are—"

"Listen, Toff. You want my help or not? I saw the white man that's helping the fugitive get away. Young thin fella, beaver hat, gray suit. That's right, isn't it? All right. I saw him hide the fugitive inside the stern hurricane lifeboat. You can go look for yourself if you want . . . only he's not there now."

"Dog bone hit all, that's what I want to know! *Where's he now?*"

"That's why I asked if he could swim. I figured he jumped boat at Bosseron's plantation."

"Bosseron's? That's thirty-some miles downriver! And this boat don't make no scheduled stop at Bosseron's."

"It did this morning," Tack lied. "Because we had Bosseron's mud clerk aboard and we let him ashore. Now if that white man who's helping the fugitive *knew* that you were on to them when they boarded this boat in New Orleans, he'd have enough sense to figure you'd be waiting for them here at Dillsburg, wouldn't he? So I figure he slipped the fugitive over the side at Bosseron's."

"Yeah," Beeker muttered, "it figgers. Okay, Tack, thanks."

"Don't mention it," Tack said casually, turning away. When he looked back he saw Beeker scurrying up the companionway to the hurricane deck. The slave chaser wasn't about to take Tack's word for it; he was going to check that lifeboat himself. Tack grinned and went up to the texas.

25

Captain Pennypacker was sitting at the table in the cuddy and the white-aproned texas tender was serving him iced coffee.

"Wasn't that Toff Beeker I seen you talking to, Tack?"

"Yes, Cap. He's after a fugitive slave that ran away from a breaking camp. Toff thought the fugitive might be aboard us."

"Huh! Hope he don't catch him. I don't like Beeker or his business or them breaking camps. I ain't any abolitionist, Tack, but there's some things about this system we got down here that sticks in my craw. It's getting too far ahead of us. Someday it's going to double back and hit us like a boomerang."

Tack helped himself to a lemon tart. The captain's prophetic thought didn't unsettle his complacency.

"Well, it doesn't really matter, does it? I mean *if* it happens, it'll be way off in the future sometime, after we're gone."

Captain Pennypacker studied him for a blank moment.

"When you're older, Tack, you'll wake up all at once and realize the future you was talking about *yesterday* is here today—spang on top of you. Time has a funny way of catching up to us like that."

Dillsburg was behind them and evening, as soft as a prayer, was creeping over the forest, the farms, and the endless river. Here and there along the distant darkling banks the woods grew spangled with light signals as each little home lit its lamp, shutting out the encroaching night, closing in on its isolated family life. A dog cut loose about something and then another and another picked it up and they filled the twilight with their sad trombone bay. But it was far away and hollow, as if they were barking down a well.

Tack felt almighty pleased with himself. It had tickled

26

him pink to put one over on Beeker, and the cream of the jest was that he was now going to cement Amos' loyalty with Beeker's money!

He figured that by the time Beeker rode all the way down to Bosseron's and wasted a few hours snooping around, and finally realized he was on a wild-goose chase, and then had to ride all the way upriver again, the *Anthony Wayne* would be at Baton Rouge, and Joe would be long gone on his path to freedom.

The firemen appeared demonlike as they sweated away before the fiercely glaring row of furnaces, and Joe looked up and gave Tack a big white grin. He seemed to be enjoying himself well enough. Maybe that was all it took to make a man like Joe happy; it wasn't work he rebelled against, but rather working in bondage.

Tack didn't see Amos anywhere around. He signaled to Guy Perrez, the second engineer. "Amos off duty?"

Guy spat at one of the huge overhead boilers and the spurt of tobacco popped like a little bomb when it struck the hot iron.

"Off the boat, is what," he said indifferently.

"How's that?"

"You heerd me, Tacky. Skipper finally up 'n' did her. Kicked old Amos plumb off at Dillsburg today."

"Kicked him off!" Tack cried. "At Dillsburg!"

"Ain't I jest said so? Seems Amos got aholt a some money somehow, so he went trompin' up to the saloon to buy hisself a gutful a redeye. You know how careless Amos always is with them cindery boots a hisn? Went trackin' up a storm all along the promenade like a cow walkin' out a mud. Pennypacker near to had a blue fit when he seen his precious deck thataway. That was the end a Amos."

Apprehension leaped into Tack's brain and started hopping up and down, jibbering in his head like an excited ape.

"Thanks, Guy," he said weakly.

27

He went up to the boiler deck and down the corridor to Hank Warnell's stateroom and knocked on the door.

"Let me in. It's Tackett."

Hank stopped smiling when he saw the strained look on Tack's face.

"What's wrong? Has something happened to Joe?"

Tack sat on the edge of the bunk and told Hank about Amos.

"You think this Amos will cause trouble then?" Hank said.

"Bet on it. He's a spiteful little scut. He'll want to get back at the captain and the *Anthony Wayne*. Also he's real greedy about money. He's bound to put in a claim for the reward."

"But he'd be implicating himself in the crime if he did," Hank reasoned. "After all, he took money from you to help Joe escape."

"He could make a deal with Toff Beeker. For a price he'd tell Beeker how I tricked him and tell him that Joe's still aboard the *Anthony Wayne*. All Beeker cares about is catching Joe. He'd keep his mouth shut about the hand Amos had in it."

"I've involved you in quite a mess, haven't I?" Hank said.

"My own fault," Tack said. "I tried to play it too foxy. I should have known better than to deal with Amos."

"Well, I'm sorry, Tack. I didn't mean to get you in trouble."

For once Tack didn't say, "Well, it doesn't really matter," because it mattered a great deal. There was a $500 fine for aiding fugitive slaves, and lately—since the South had become so concerned over the Underground Railway to the North—a six-month jail sentence was also being imposed. It meant that he was through as a steamboat pilot, through with the Mississippi River, too. In short, he was suddenly a fugitive himself.

"What do you suggest?" Hank asked.

28

"Well, you can count your chickens that Beeker or the law or both will be waiting for us when we reach Baton Rouge. So—we've got to jump ship between here and there. And sooner the better."

He got up and went to the door, saying:

"Now look. Back at the stern of the lower deck we keep some lifeboats for the firemen. They're flimsy little contraptions and two men can ship them easy. You go down there and wait for me. I have something to do topside first. Then I'll get Joe and join you. See you."

The cuddy was deserted. Tack rounded up a quill and a piece of paper and dashed down a brief note To Whom It May Concern:

> I hereby admit that I was the one who helped the fugitive slave called Joe escape. Neither Captain Pennypacker nor any member of the *A. Wayne*'s crew had a hand in it or knew anything about it . . . except Chief Engineer Amos Rynd who hid Joe in his black gang for $10.

> F. B. Tackett

He tucked the note in his pocket and went up to the pilothouse. Old Ben was in a fairly hopping mood of temper. He hit the brass cuspidor a wet lick that set it back on its round heel.

"Where in tarnation you been? Am I learnin' you how to lazy about in your bunk all the livelong day or am I learnin' you how to be a steamboat pilot!"

Tack smiled. He was going to miss this old reprobate.

"I'll take the wheel for a spell, Ben."

"*Quite* a spell!" Ben fumed. "All night, in fact. So's I kin git me some readin' time in!"—the mention of which sidetracked his temper. He picked up the *Ladies' Repository* excitedly.

"Say—say, Tack, you know what Fanny went and did?

29

I managed to slip me in a couple more pages while we was sliding up Ralls Reach, which even a blind man could pilot through at midnight with the shades drawn. Anyhow, she went and remembered that there pistol! Yeah, and you that thinks you know so much more'n her!"

"That's fine, Ben," Tack said. "But let's not talk about Fanny now. I want to tell you some—"

A gosh-awful bellow came from the dark shore.

"*Anthony Wayne!* Hello the *Wayne!*"

Muttering peevishly to himself, Ben sprang to one of the side windows and threw it open, yelling into the night.

"Who's skylarkin' out there! What fool is that?"

"This is Sheriff Poole! Come ashore in the name of the law! I'm going to board you!"

"You'll board a whole river a water if you try!" Ben yelled, though he clanged his bell for half-speed. "I ain't putting in for no prankster at my age. Show a light if you be who you say you be!"

Tack clutched the palm-worn wheel spokes and let out his breath. It had come sooner than he had expected. Amos hadn't lost any time. And the fact that the lawman was Sheriff Poole explained a lot. Everybody along the river knew that Poole was as grabby as a hog when it came to money. Tack was willing to bet his right boot that the sheriff had his hand in the reward pie somehow.

A light flared in the vastness of the night, like a desperate signal from shipwrecked men on a lonely island, and then a lamp was raised among the dozing live oaks on the shore. Tack saw Sheriff Poole, a nameless constable, Toff Beeker and Amos Rynd.

"Say, Tack, you reckon they're after them two Spanishers we got aboard? Them riverboat gamblers? They're a danger-ous lot. Killed a man up at Natchez last year. Least that's what folks say."

"No, Ben, they're not after the gamblers," Tack said. He

30

let Ben take the wheel. He drew the folded note from his pocket.

"Give 'em this, Ben. It'll explain everything. And—well, I've got to go now, got to say so long."

Ben didn't open the note. He stared at Tack.

"Tacky, you in trouble, boy?" he asked quietly.

"Something like that. Anyhow, I want to thank you for all the trouble you've taken to teach me the river. Guess I've always been a pain in the neck to you, but you've been a real friend to me."

"Ah, Tack, Tack," the old man said softly. He really seemed broken about it. He put out his hand. Tack took it and grinned.

"I hope everything comes out all right for Fanny," he said.

"Tack!" Ben called after him. "You give them Mexicans heck for me, hear?"

Mexicans? Tack wondered, walking quickly along the deck. What ever gave old Ben the idea that he was going to strike for Texas? He shrugged and went bounding down the companionway.

3

WE'LL SHOW 'EM, WON'T
WE, TACK?

Tack walked briskly across the furnace deck, his face set in a blank mask. "Need to borrow one of your hands for a minute, Guy," he said to the engineer.

"Help yourself, Tack. What's the law up to out there, huh?"

"Beats me. You"—pointing at the wide-eyed Joe—"c'mon."

Joe tailed Tack out of the light and into the shadows thrown by the bulging mass of the boilers, on back to the misty stern. Praise the Lord the swamp was smoking tonight. It would give them cover. Hank was waiting for them nervously.

"I shipped the boat as soon as I heard the law call," he said.

Joe chattered. "Is the law gonna kotch me now, Marse Hank? Are they gonna shoot pore ol'—"

"Shut up, can't you!" Tack snapped. "We've got enough

trouble on our hands without you going to panic. Get into the boat."

Hank hauled the boat alongside by its painter. It rocked in the black water under the stalled *Anthony Wayne*'s dark counter.

"Don't talk, don't make noise," Tack warned them.

They scrambled into the boat and Tack cast off the line.

"Ease away with the oars," he whispered. "Bear on around the steamboat and keep to the shore. I'll show you where to go."

Cautiously, quietly, they slipped along the portside of the steamboat, the great mass of the steamer looming threateningly above them, glistening white and ghostlike in the swamp mist. Tack could hear angry voices from somewhere on the boiler deck.

"Where are we going?" Hank whispered.

"Bear portside—to the left. The Jameson Cutoff is just ahead."

"Jimson Cutoff!" Joe gasped. "Marse Tack, you cain't mean to take us in that hanty ol' place!"

"What's wrong with it?" Hank asked anxiously.

Nothing, Tack explained. Just one of the river's little jokes. . . .

Once there had been an enormous elbow bend here in the river, but—as was usual with the Mississippi, which was forever shortening its rily road to the sea—the river had sliced a shortcut for itself smack through the center of the elbow, thereby chopping off 25 miles. Which turned the outer point of the elbow into an island. But not for long. Because with the passing of the years the old bend began to fill up with flotsam and jetsam and saplings, so that now it was a boat trap.

Legend was that a steamer had blundered in there by mistake one swamp-misty night and never had been able to find its way out. Backwoods superstition had it that the specter steamer was still drifting forlornly around in the dis-

33

mal ghost-ridden old bend. Some folks claimed you could even hear the plaintive wail of her leadsman on certain gloomy nights, calling:

N-o bottom! N-o bottom . . . !

"It's only a legend, Joe," Tack said.

"Man, I don't care who its name. I ain't *about* to take me down an' shake *han's* with it!"

Tack, in his present state of mind, was holding his temper on a mighty short leash.

"Now listen to me, Joe. And you listen good. I don't want—"

A shout sprang from the receding *Anthony Wayne.*

"Hi, Sheriff! They're making off in a rowboat! *There! There!*"

It sounded like that little scut Amos. Tack yelled at Hank.

"C'mon! Put your blame Bostonian back into it! *Move those oars!* Snatch her! Snatch her! *Joe*—get in there and help!"

Something went *pak* from the steamer's boiler deck, and a pencil-thin spurt of water shot up off the rowboat's starboard quarter.

"Row, boy, row!" Tack hissed. "That fool's opened fire!"

Pak pak pak!

Heyday! That sheriff must be packing a five-shot revolver.

"Joe! Will you lend a hand on—" Tack shut up, staring gawk-eyed at Joe, who was standing up and already leaning toward the stern.

"Man, 'tween hanty rivers an' pistol shoots, this ain't no place fo Mammy Tope's li'l boy Joe! I'm gittin'!"

And he did, too. Just like that and all at once—throwing himself overboard with a black crash of water. Gone.

"Can he swim?" Tack wondered.

"I guess he can!" Hank cried. "Least I *hope* he can!"

They pulled into the deserted bend and Hank relaxed on

34

the oars, looking up and around. It was a ghastly place in the misty night, all shapes vague and distorted. The cypress stumps upreared around them, garlanded with moss beard and swamp smoke, and the creeper vines hung down from the water oaks like the tentacles of a mindless, soulless predator.

Tack shivered and glanced over his shoulder into the damp opaque gloom. He had always heard that the place was bad, but imagination never quite has the awesomeness of stark reality. All around them now the swamp silence grew, like a dumb monster watching solemnly from the mist. Sound seemed smothered.

"Move over," he said. "We got a long row ahead of us."

"Where?"

"Clear down to the end of this place. I figure the sheriff will wait till daylight, then take one of the *Wayne*'s boats and come in here looking for us. I could be wrong, though. He might order the *Wayne* down to the end of the bend and wait there for us to come out. One way or the other, we can't just sit here."

Hank's teeth flashed in the gloom.

"I go you, Tack. Let's see which of your guesses is right."

Dawn was coming like an Indian creeping across a fallow field when Tack and Hank reached the filled-in end of the old bend. There wasn't a chance of getting the boat through that quagmire.

"Leave it," Tack said. "We'll have to strike out on foot."

It was mean going. The crosspatch maze of sticks and logs and flotsam was like a gigantic beaver dam. It took them an hour to cross over the backup. Then, soaked, disheveled, hungry and beat, they stood looking down on a ratty old keelboat nestled in the protective cove of the horseshoe bend. It was morning.

"Let's see if anyone's aboard," Tack said. "Maybe we can scare up some grub."

35

They had to jump from the bank to the deck. They walked along the port gangway to the little door in the rear of the cabin. All three of the windows were shuttered. The door was closed. Tack tried the latch. It was free. He grinned back at Hank.

"I think it's deserted."

He swung the door into the cabin darkness and started to step down and in himself . . . walking right into an Elgin cutlass pistol.

Tack had never seen a weapon like it before and he wasn't any too happy to see this one at the end of his nose. It was built like a short double-barreled horse pistol with a 12-inch blade beneath the barrels, bayonetlike. It was a naval side arm and it combined the merits of a boarding pistol and a cutlass, for hand-to-hand combat. All in all it was a bad-news weapon.

"Step one more foot, boy," a voice rasped in the shadows, "and it's the last one you'll ever take."

There's not much sense in arguing with a positive statement like that—not when two gun barrels are staring you in the eyes.

Tack swallowed and whispered, "All right. Who's moving?"

The voice in the gloom chuckled. "Smart. What're you after?"

"You take that meat-cleaver shotgun out of my face and maybe we can talk," Tack said.

"Let 'em come in, Lou," a second voice said.

The Elgin pistol dropped from Tack's face and the raspy voice said, "Sure. As long as they keep their hands high."

Considering the circumstances, it seemed like pretty good advice. Tack "reached" and stepped into the cabin. He was getting used to the dim light. The man with the pistol was a stocky rough-and-tumble sort, somewhere in his mid-forties. The other was a grinning rake-handle youth, say eighteen-nineteenish.

"My name's Nap Mitchell," the skinny boy said. "This is my pard, Lou Rose. Don't mind his rough edges—he's an old soldier."

Tack looked at the bandy-legged ex-soldier.

"What war? Eighteen-twelve?"

"Uh-uh," Louis Rose said. "Napoleonic."

That suited Tack just fine. It had been his experience that soldiers of fortune were usually ripe for any enterprise that smacked of adventure and profit. They had a casual way of winking at the law.

"My name's Tackett," he said. "This is Hank Warnell. We're in trouble with the law." He paused, looking at Mitchell and Rose, waiting for their reaction. Nap Mitchell grinned at him and Lou Rose waved his pistol toward a Franklin stove.

"Have some coffee."

"We tried to help a fugitive slave escape," Hank said. "Now the law's after us. They might show up at any minute."

"We ain't got any milk," Rose said. "Hope you like it black."

Tack relaxed. Evidently they were among friends.

Young Nap was at one of the windows. He shut it abruptly.

"They didn't speak up a second too soon," he said. "Batch of armed men coming round the bend in a rowboat."

Rose grunted and motioned toward a little door in the forward wall. "Get in there. Keep shut up."

Tack nodded and opened the door and hunched into the cramped forward hole. It was as black as the inside of a stovepipe. Hank closed the door after them, and they waited.

Outside, there was a knock of wood against wood and booted feet went clumping along the gangway and around the back and down the steps. Then a voice spoke. Sheriff Poole.

"You fellas seen anything of two boys in a rowboat?"

Tack put his eye to a crack in the bulkhead. He could make out Rose and Mitchell sitting at the table, and Poole, Beeker, Amos and the constable standing before them.

"What kind of rowboat?" Rose asked. He sipped his coffee.

"Never mind the smarties," Poole snapped. "Did you *see* 'em?"

"Uh-huh. They came by an hour ago. Only they weren't in any rowboat. It was a frigate and they fired a ten-gun salute at us. Nap here replied by tossing an empty bean can at them, and I gave 'em a spurt of tobacco juice. They seemed peeved."

"That's very funny," Sheriff Poole said. "That's really very funny. It might earn you a month in the hoosegow."

Rose drew his pistol from his belt and placed it on the table.

"On what charge?" he asked.

Poole looked at the Elgin pistol and seemed to stall somewhat.

"Listen," he said finally, "you know what happens to people that aid or abet a fugitive slave?"

"Uh-huh," Rose said. "Five-hundred-dollar fine. I ain't got it. Or five cents. You're wasting your time."

Toff Beeker nudged the sheriff. "Let's have a look around."

Rose set his cup down. "Not on my boat," he told them. "Not without my say-so."

"C'mon," Beeker insisted. "There's only two of 'em."

Rose tapped the butt of the pistol with his forefinger.

"Nap, did I load this thing with buckshot or ball? I seem to have forgot."

"Both," Nap said.

Sheriff Poole diplomatically moved to a fresh issue.

"Where'd you get this keelboat?"

"My grampa built her," Rose said. "He was Noah's apprentice. I got a couple of elephants and kangaroos up forward."

"Where do you think you're going in it?" Poole asked doggedly.

"To Texas," Nap answered, grinning. "Want to come along?"

"Are you going to search this scow or are you goan let 'em sass you all day?" Toff Beeker demanded of the sheriff.

Nap rose and shifted over to the stove, dropping his hand on the haft of a wood-chopping ax. Rose toyed with his pistol.

Amos Rynd cleared his throat and started easing himself toward the aft door. The constable eased right along with him.

"C'mon," Amos said in a small voice. "They ain't here."

Sheriff Poole glanced at Toff Beeker.

"I'm looking for a fugitive slave, Toff, not for trouble. I don't know about you." He spun on his heel and made for the door.

Beeker stalled indecisively. Lou Rose started to stand up.

"I don't think I invited you aboard my boat, mister," he said to Beeker. "Maybe you best get along with your friends."

Beeker said something low and dirty, then he got out. Rose sat down again as Nap went to close the rear door. Tack and Hank squeezed back into the cabin.

"Thanks," Tack said.

Nap grinned and said, "How about that coffee now?"

"Are you really going to Texas?" Hank asked Lou Rose.

"Quickest way we can find. Nap here came all the way from Georgia. We met up along the road."

"How did you come by this keelboat?"

Nap opened his mouth but Rose cut in promptly: "Found it."

"Found it?" Hank echoed wonderingly. "A boat like this?"

"That's what I said, son," Rose said flatly.

Tack gave Hank a warning nudge. It wasn't a safe practice to ask too many questions on the Mississippi, where every man had his own special style of doing things, of getting along.

"I'm for Texas, too," Hank said. "But Tack has other plans."

Rose shifted around on his bench and studied Tack.

"Like what? Hiding in one of the swamps for a year from the law? Better throw in with us, son. We'll make up a party. Ain't no law nor nobody going to bother you if we all stick together."

"What are your plans, exactly?" Tack asked.

"Pretty simple. We're going up the Red River to Alexandria. Then we'll catch a stage into Texas."

"Cost money," Tack said. "Me 'n' Hank are somewhat short."

"You got no problem, boy," Lou Rose said. "We'll sell this boat in Alexandria. That'll see our stage fares. I told you we would stick together."

Nap grinned encouragingly. "How about it?"

"We'll show 'em, won't we, Tack?" Hank prompted him.

Texas, Tack thought. War. Well, maybe it wouldn't really come to that. Maybe it would be called off by the time he and the others got there. Texas was a long way off. Yeah. Might even be fun. A new sort of adventure. Yeah . . .

"All right," he said. "If the rest of you are set on it, I'll throw in. Can't lose anything, I guess."

"That's right," Nap said with a grin. "Only our lives."

And then they all laughed, and Tack said, "That's right, that's all."

They actually laughed.

41

4

STAGE TO BEXAR

Everywhere now men were on the move. They came by steamboat, keelboat, schooner and raft. You saw them going by on coaches, wagons and horses. Sometimes you saw them on foot, bumming it along the best way they could. They went in gangs and by twos and threes and some went alone. Most of them were armed, and the conglomeration of weapons was a thing of wonder.

Man-tall Tower muskets that had served their apprenticeship in the Revolutionary War and that hit like a brick slammed against a barn; long rifles that could pick out a fox's eye at 400 paces without harming a hair on his pelt; French carbines and double-barreled shotguns, squirrel guns and fowling pieces; Granddaddy's old horse pistol and Pa's cap'n'ball and Uncle Tope's pepper-box revolver. All for Texas.

Ex-army officers and soldiers of fortune and all that motley crew of let's-see-what's-beyond-the-next-hill adventurers; all ages, but mostly boys—city boys and farm boys and even a driver boy from the Erie Canal; and backwoodsmen

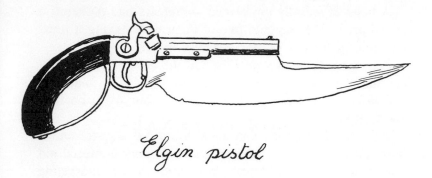

Elgin pistol

and the usual assortment of grinning country yahoos and professional men, too—a lawyer, a doctor, an ex-justice of the peace. All going to become something that they had hardly even heard of two months before. Texans.

Alexandria was a rampant town. The storekeepers were singing happy songs and jacking up their prices quicker than a man could spit and turn around. Business was booming along like a brass cannon. Lou Rose made a deal on the keelboat and came away grinning like the devil on a holiday . . . until they looked up a stage line and talked to the ticket agent.

The fare he quoted nearly unhinged the four adventurers.

"And that ain't all," he told them. "We can't carry you 'less you have your own fodder and guns. With all these men dribbling into Texas, those bushwhacking redskins are having a heyday. Ever' male passenger's got to be prepared to help defend the stage."

Well, that was that. They had enough money for fares and food but not enough left over with which to buy weapons.

Tack shrugged and turned to stare at the milling traffic

in the circuslike street. A crude hand-printed banner said:

LIBERTY   INDEPENDENCE   VOLUNTEER NOW
TAKE TEXAS

A band of weirdly uniformed volunteers had gathered a crowd across the way and one of them was making a rousing and somewhat romantic soapbox speech:

". . . and we hereby *declare* that we have left every endearment in the *You*-nited States of America to maintain and *defend* our brethren, at the peril of our lives, liberties and fortunes!"

The crowd whooped and some fool fired a pistol and a horse hitched to a shay stampeded and a poor confused old granny who had just stepped outside to do her marketing nearly had herself trampled into the mud. Down the street a band had formed before the hotel and now the fife and drum cut loose with *Hail, the Conquering Hero Comes! Tra-la.*

"Say," Tack said, "who's the Conquering Hero supposed to be?"

The ticket agent was appalled by Tack's ignorance.

"Ain't you heard? Davy Crockett's down there. Him 'n' some Tennessee friends started down this way to do a little peaceful hunting. But everywhere they went folks immediately a-sumed Davy was coming to help the Texans. Now it seems he's being herded right into Texas."

"You mean *Colonel* Crockett—the Congressman?" Hank asked.

"*The* Davy Crockett—the famous frontiersman?" Tack asked.

"Is there any other Colonel Davy Crockett?" the agent wondered.

"C'mon," Lou Rose said. "I want to see that man."

There was a dandy crowd in the hotel's saloon and the overflow was filling up the lobby. This didn't phase Rose. He shouldered his way through the sardinelike throng, turn-

44

ing up a tight little smile at any person who frowned at him, and kept on shoving.

That was one of the things about Lou Rose that bothered Tack. He was a pushy man. He'd give you a shove and a smile, as if daring you to do something about it. There was a streak of the hardheaded bully in him that Tack didn't admire.

Mumbling apologies as he tried to thread himself after Rose, Tack heard Crockett's booming voice.

". . . so when my Whig constituents—that's a name they use in Washington fer a fella who claims he's your best supporter even if he's got to put a knife in your back to prove hit—when they turned agin me and voted me out a business, I told them that as far as I was concerned *they* could go to hell—*I'd* go to Texas."

The crowd simply loved him. His peculiar syntax and woodsy humor delighted them all hollow. They ripped a roar of laughter and those who had room enough to do it in slapped their knees.

Tack was a little disappointed. Davy didn't look like the brimstone-eating wildcat that all America loved. He was picturesque enough in his Indian moccasins and buckskin shirt, with the frozen face of the raccoon on his cap glaring defiantly like a masked bandit—but he was getting on to fifty and his 200 pounds had started to bulge around the seams and his face was the face of a warmhearted kindly old farmer.

A curious man, Crockett; he had decided to create and live his own legend in his own time, and so he had become (possibly) the most outlandish liar ever produced in America. He liked to affect a deep-rooted backwoods ignorance, pretending that he could neither read nor write when actually he was very proficient at both. He hired ghost writers to spread fantastic stories that only the most gullible and infantile minds could swallow without getting their tongues caught in their cheeks.

Typical of the created legends were the whoppers about Davy killing six braves in one day, or shooting 47 bears in one month, or riding alligators bareback, or grinning a bear into total panic, or whipping his weight in wildcats before breakfast.

"The reason I come down here," Davy was telling the crowd, "was to see fer myself if hit's really true that a family of eight kin live off one Texas watermelon fer a week, and then use the seeds to load in their guns and shoot Mexicans with."

The crowd whooped again, as Rose squeezed up to Crockett.

"Speaking of Texas, Colonel," Rose said. "I've got three volunteers with me, and we've got the cash to get us to Texas all right, but not enough to arm ourselves with. And the rule is nobody can go to Texas these days unless he's armed like a fort. Thought maybe you could give us a hand."

"Say, wait a minute, Lou!" Hank called. "Speak for yourself, will you? *I* don't beg."

Hank was beet-red with outraged embarrassment, but Tack secretly wished he would keep his mouth shut. If you couldn't get to Texas without guns, and if Rose was the only one of the team who had the unmitigated gall to get the guns for them, then Tack figured that he and Hank and Nap should let well enough alone.

Rose, however, knew his man. Crockett wasn't the slightest bit unsettled by the startling and nervy request.

"Is *that* all you need, brother? Guns? Shucks. I got a party of a dozen Tennessee hunters with me and we got so many weapons along we're near to shootin' each other full a holes ever' time we try to crowd around the same dinner table!"

He turned to Hank. "There ain't no question of begging here, son. Shucks, we're *all* going to Bexar to fight, ain't we? Can't do no fightin' without guns, can you? Well, me

46

'n' my friends is fixin' to loan you some of our spare parts. We can settle up later on. Abner, you 'n' Lindsy see what you can scare up for these volunteers."

"Colonel, let me stand you a drink," Rose said.

"Don't mind if you do, brother. Don't mind a-tall. Course you realize that this pap they serve here ain't beans to what we drink back home. In Tennessee we mix dee-luded gunpowder 'n' panther spit with our likker . . ."

The colonel was starting another of his outlandish tales.

"I don't care what you say," Hank said angrily, as he and Nap and Tack stood by the loading stage. "But *I* say Rose assumes too much. He overreaches the bounds of proper behavior."

"Well, it doesn't really matter, does it?" Tack said. "At least we have the guns now, and we can get to Texas. After all, Hank, you were the one who was so hot about getting to Bexar."

"Yes. But there's a right way of going and a wrong way. And as far as I can see Rose invariably picks all the wrong ways." He turned to Nap. "Did he really steal that keelboat, as I suspect?"

Nap grinned. "Ask him, Hank, why don't you? Lou can think up a lie quicker than Crockett."

The driver, short and bandy-legged, came out of the office spitting tobacco juice right and left—already swearing a blue streak about horses and harness and coaches and passengers and other vague references that were mystifying to Tack—and yelled:

"All right, boys, load up! Load up! Ain't got all blame day."

The stagecoach was the usual Concord type, the kind which was shortly and wholeheartedly to be adopted by the West. It would seat four comfortably and six in a pinch. Today's load called for eight.

There were two female passengers—a fat old battle-ax

47

and her shy-eyed daughter—a farm boy from Illinois, Robert Brown, and a runaway printer's apprentice from Arkansas, Richardson Perry. Plus the four adventurers from the Mississippi River.

Rose stumped out of the office, bearing over his shoulder a double-barreled shotgun that the Tennesseans had given him.

"Gonna cram us all in there?" he wanted to know.

"No, I ain't," the driver said and spat downwind. "You can ride shotgun up front with me. One a you other boys will have to ride topside with the spare baggage."

They agreed to swap off, spell each other: Nap riding up top first, then Hank, and so on. Tack wedged himself in between Hank and Richardson Perry. The Simpsons (Battle-ax and daughter) sat across from them with Robert Brown, facing front.

The whip went *spamp*! and the driver yelled *Hee-YAH! Josie! Pete!* and the trace chains started to go jinglety-jank as the team dug in, lunged forward, and the coach took off with an abrupt jar.

They were off. Texas-bound.

Am I really sitting here in a stagecoach for the first time in my life? Tack wondered. *In a strange land? Going to an even stranger place? To a war that in no way concerns me?*

Funny the way things work out, he thought, staring at the brown-turning landscape sliding rapidly by the windows. Very funny.

Twilight was easing itself across the prairie as stealthly as a war-painted savage creeping from bush to bush, when Tack was roused from a restless doze by Lou Rose's harsh voice.

"Time to turn about, Hank!"

Tack blinked his eyes and sat up, looking around. The Battle-ax was staring at him with haughty disapproval. The

48

young daughter was watching him covertly. He yawned and winked at her.

"Um-*hmm!*" The Battle-ax cleared her throat threateningly.

"Move a leg, Hank!" Rose's voice sounded again.

"Why don't you relax, Lou?" Tack heard Hank call from on top of the coach roof. "We're working out our relay system all right by ourselves."

Tack forgot about the irate Battle-ax. He wished that Hank would make an effort to get along with Rose. Granted that Rose was deeply ingrained with the soldier of fortune's usual leader complex; still, he knew all the tricks of the trade, things that were a complete mystery to Tack and Hank and Nap. He was a good man to have along in a pinch.

"Excuse me," Tack muttered, working himself loose from Nap and Perry. It was his turn topside. Somehow or other he managed to step on the Battle-ax's right foot as he got up.

"*Oh!* Clumsy!"

"Sorry, ma'am," he mumbled, rocking with the precarious bounce and joggle of the coach. "Crowded in here." He glanced at the daughter. She was ducking a smile under a lace hankerchief.

Hank swung down from above, coming legs-first through the open top half of the left-side door.

"How's the weather up there?" Tack asked him.

"Getting almighty cold. You'd think that the Texans and Mexicans could pick a better season to start a war in."

Tack put his back to the right-hand door and leaned outside, reaching up and grabbing the baggage rack, and then hauled himself out the door and up and over the edge of the roof and settled himself belly-flat among the boxes and bags and blanket rolls.

He looked at the driver and Rose jouncing on their hard

49

seat as the team charged way-hey along, the rolling prairie falling away on either hand. The driver spat a jawful and the backdraft caught it and splattered it. Tack yelled *Hey! Hey!* wiping his face. Rose looked back and grinned at him.

"Hank got the same dose, Tack!"

Then the driver glanced back. "Sorry—forgot!"

Hank had left his rifle up on the roof. It was a percussion cap-and-hammer job, similar to the famous Kentucky rifle. Tack checked to see that it was primed for action. Hank had all the avidity of a soldier but not the instincts, the earthy know-how.

He looked back at their dust-spun wake. The twilight seemed intent on chasing them, following after with silent pink and gray shadows. The coach's hurrahing rush had spooked the inhabitants of the scrubby mesquite-clad hills humping up in the west. With a snort of fear a doe leaped away, crashing through the sagebrush. A prowling coyote fled down a cholla cañon, and all the wild twilight hunters scattered into the dense shelters of manzanita and buck-thorn and catclaw.

From somewhere on the hillside came the coughing cry of a mountain lion, and at the sound the dusky prairie became as still as death, except for the jobbity-jobbity of the rolling coach.

Tack lowered his head to scratch his nose—and froze.

The Cherokees came right out of nowhere. Belting out of the granite rocks and over the sego-clad rumples in the prairie on their barebacked war ponies, shattering the fabric of the milkish-pink sky with their war whoops.

There must have been fifty-sixty of them. They came bucketing across the mesa with their trade rifles and con-fiscated carbines and primitive bows and arrows. And how they managed those half-outlawed nags with only a sketchy bit of rope—which was neither proper bridle nor halter but only a loop about the nag's lower jaw—and without hardly

bothering to hold onto the rope reins, was a wonderful mystery.

They came right and left, running with an abandoned air of wild-born freedom, parallel to the stage, and then started cutting in.

They went EEE-YUYU-YUUU! firing and loading as they came, the bullets hitting *whock-whock* against the coach and the brittle-bright arrows landing *tthok-tthok* in the doors and panels and boot.

Tack panned his rifle with an incoming savage and fired and the Indian went right on over the swerving horse's head and hit the ground in an explosion of dust, his pony swinging up its head and backrolling its right eye and galloping on out of there as if it was being paid for it.

Then Rose, who had waited until his mark came driving in toward the off-leader horse, let loose with one barrel and that Cherokee and his mount went down in a flurry of kicking legs and arms and hoofs; while the driver pegged one vicious stone after another at the going-away rumps of his frantic team, yelling:

"*HEE-YAH! HEE-YAH!* Josie! Pete! Go you spavined *hombres*!"

Then Hank and Nap and Perry and Brown opened up with everything they had from the windows, and Tack, reloading, saw one-two Cherokees spill onto the ground.

Then Rose swung his shotgun over the driver's back and blasted point-blank at a Cherokee who was coming at the nigh leader so fast and savage that you wouldn't think anything as puny as a mere shotgun charge could stop that much determination of purpose. But it did—piling the redskin ten feet from his veering pony.

Tack raised and ducked quick as an arrow needled the air and landed *th-ok* in a hatbox, and raised again and sighted down on an Indian who was urging his pony right up to the rear boot, and fired, the gun going *POWM* in his hands, and thinking:

Lord, they're beautiful! They're beautiful the way they ride!

And they were, too—coming after and in at the flying coach, forcing those ponies on and on with their bucking knees, dumping in powder from their horns and reversing their rifles to bring the barrels to their mouths, spitting a ball down them and cocking on the overswing, and sighting and firing. And to look at them you would think that they and their mounts were one, welded together in purpose and understanding as they came pounding and war-whooping along, the legs of the ponies reaching, throwing, going, finding and slashing and thundering the earth.

"*HEE-YAH!* Josie! Blast your spade soul! *Gee-up* thar!" The driver cast his head around, taking a quick look from side to side, and grinned from ear to ear.

"Who says I can't run 'em! We're calamity on wheels!

We're the be-all and end-all of prairie pushers when we turn loose! Hi! Pete! Show 'em heels, son! Show 'em horseshoes silver 'n' bright 'n' long gone! *HEE-YAH!*"

He was a little mad. They all were, red and white man alike.

The coach went swerving in and out of the mesquite clumps, hitting the high spots as it bounced over the potholes and chuckholes, slamming good-gosh along for the setting sun.

The Cherokees started to drop back, turning their ponies to the right and left, lowering their weapons. The last following Indian was a sachem, Tack figured, because he wore a tall war bonnet and carried an eagle-feathered spear. Tack took a sight on him, but his finger stalled on the trigger as the sachem brought his pony to a sliding halt in the dust-whipped trail and raised his spear in a savage salute to the stagecoach.

Tack came to his knees and raised his rifle above his head. For a static bouncing, dusty moment they were like that, the red man and the white man. Then the Indian lowered his spear and turned his horse away. Tack brought his gun down, staring back.

"*O-oh!* My saints! Are they gone?" The Battle-ax's wail came up to Tack. And he heard Nap's ecstatic cry:

"Hey bo, that was really something! What I mean *something!*"

And Rose was crowing away like a rooster in a henyard:

"I got two of 'em! You see it? Don't tell me the shotgun won't be the ruling weapon in future wars!"

And still Tack knelt there staring back at the diminishing figure of the war-bonneted savage.

"Well done, Chief," he whispered.

5

JUST ONE OF THOSE THINGS THAT
HAPPEN IN WAR

Bexar.

Its full name was San Antonio de Bexar, but everyone liked to shortcut it to simply Bexar. It was not the hub of Texas (Brownwood probably was) but it was certainly the key town, because it stood at the crossroads of the Texas panhandle.

In its heyday Bexar had been the provincial capital under the Spanish rule, but with the dawning of Mexican independence it had become a neglected falling-to-ruin outpost. Within a decade half its population had decamped. A few Americanos had drifted in and put down roots: among them a legendary man known as Jim Bowie . . .

There wasn't much to the place: a crosspatch of straggling streets; two central squares called the Main Plaza and the Military Plaza, both dominated by the San Fernando Church; a disorderly scramble of flat-roofed adobe houses; the little dun-colored San Antonio River glinting and gurgling along the eastern hem of the town, and—across the river and in a splendid isolation of decay and abandonment —a stone-walled mission built in 1750. The Alamo.

Tack and his friends got off the coach at the outskirts of town. The sporadic slam and *pak-pak* of guns sounded in the distance, and the driver didn't waste any time in wishing them good luck and in wheeling his team around and getting himself out of there.

Tack was aware of a disturbing sense of something gone wrong.

"What's going on here?" Rose asked, grabbing a rangy-looking backwoodsman who was shuffling through a tent area south of town.

"Hang-up, son," the woodsy man said. "Old Gin'ril Cós has got hisself bottled up in town and in that air Alamo. Us Texans has got 'em fenced, but we ain't got us no real leadership. Not like we had us at N'awleans when old Andy whupped the British." He spat, making a brown dirtball in the dust, and pointed.

"See that banner flappin' over yon?"

Over the rag-and-taggle collection of dilapidated tents and makeshift huts waved a white cloth decorated with black paint. It bore a lone star and a cannon and the words COME AND TAKE IT.

"Steve Austin led us fum Gonzales under that flag in October. Five hunnert of us. Since then we been bogged down here like a broke-leggit cow in a sump hole, sufferin' fum desertions 'n' smallpox ever' day. Then Austin, he took and left us to go dig up some support in the *You*-nited States. Gin'ril Burleson took command. But he ain't got no more fight in him than a newbornt pup dog."

"What about that Travis fellow?" Hank asked.

"The colonel? He went rippin' about fer a few weeks, burnin' grass and catchin' Mex hosses. Then he pulled out, too. Went over to San Felipe to help set up a Pro-visional Government of Texas. Way I see hit is, this here war's going

55

to be a matter a patience: to see which side kin bore t'other side to death fust."

Tack was secretly pleased. This was the kind of war he approved of. Nobody dies. But Hank and Nap looked let down. Not so with Lou Rose. He was a seasoned campaigner. He took things the way they came.

"C'mon," he said. "We'll find some kind of shebang to bunk in, then I'll scout up some rations."

"Well, what will we do after that?" Hank asked restlessly.

"Do?" Rose looked surprised. "Why, we'll do what every soldier does whenever he gets the chance to. Flake out on our backs and get some sleep. C'mon. You'll catch on to war after a while."

The guns slammed and the siege dragged on like a weary old ox plodding about a gristmill. Desertions were commonplace; the sick list grew; the idle troops became disgruntled and fistfights were frequent. A man called Conway went after a Sherod Dover with a knife and killed him, and the Texans from Captain Coleman's company hanged Conway on a pecan tree. Rose went over to watch.

Tack and his friends were living in a dismal board and tarp arrangement that threatened to collapse with the first wind. He and Hank were lazying around inside on their blankets when Rose returned from the hanging.

"Say," he told them, "it was sweet! They had him on a bareback nag, see? His hands tied behind. Then one of 'em yells *Yah*! And they bring down the switch and that nag goes cannonballing out of there, and for a second it looks like Conway is going away with the horse. Until he runs to the end of that rope. And then *sssp*!"

"Shut up!" Hank snarled, sitting up, his face tight and apoplectic. "We don't want to hear about it. Just shut up."

Rose closed his mouth and looked at Hank.

"What did you say, boy?"

56

"You heard me. I said shut up."

Tack stood up and stepped in front of Rose.

"Take it easy. Both of you. We're friends, aren't we? We all agreed to stick together, didn't we?"

Rose nodded shortly, so did Hank. Hank said, "Sorry, Lou," and Rose said, "Forget it."

The inactivity was beginning to tell on all of them. Something was going to have to break. And soon. Then it did, on the 2nd of December. Nap came racing back from headquarters wild with excitement.

"Two American residents just escaped from Bexar," he said. "Sam Maverick and John Smith. They say the Mexicans are low on chow and ammo and are just about as fed up as we are. Maverick's trying to get old Burleson to attack right off! He smuggled out some maps and he's got a plan of attack all figgered out!"

They snatched up their guns and rushed for the outdoors. Action at last!

But General Burleson had news for them. He couldn't seem to bring himself to give the order to advance. He hung fire for two solid days, not able to say Yes, not able to say No; while his officers shouted and argued themselves blue and pointed at the maps and at Bexar and at their own troops who were mighty near the edge of mutiny. And still Burleson stalled indecisively.

Until finally a sun-cured old plainsman called Ben Milam reached his limit and blew up right in the command tent.

"By juckies, Gin'ril, I've had me a bellyful of this namby-pamby talk! If you won't take 'em into that town, *I* will!" He charged out of the tent and confronted the troops impatiently waiting for news.

"Boys, who will come with old Ben Milam into San Antonio?"

Two hundred and forty weapons were raised in the air and a mighty shout roared through the camp. If he was ready to go, then by grab so were they!

57

Hank slapped Tack on the back. "We're really going to do it this time, Tack! We're going to fight the Mexicans at last!"

Yeah, Tack thought bleakly, at last. . . .

Dawn . . . and men moving across a broken field, gathering momentum, coming to a run. Soldiers without uniforms, in nondescript old clothes starched stiff with dirt, baggy-kneed. Tough frontier faces, ageless, bearded and leathery; fresh new faces, young, beardless and spanking bright; raw eyes, wide and eager, full of fervor, glory. Grenades, round and black, bouncing inside shirts, joggling against hairy and hairless chests; long rifles with bayonets winking in the pale pink spreading light; swords, cold and long and straight, pointing the way. Texans in the making, advancing. . . .

Tack was running with Lou Rose. He had lost track of Hank and Nap. Heavy, skin-bruising grenades were bouncing inside their shirts; glowing cigars were clenched in their teeth. Tack was following Rose's example. Rose fought like a European. He scorned rifles and bayonets; used shotguns and grenades for close fighting. European grenadiers carried lighted punks for their bombs, but Rose said a cigar was more handy.

The long disorderly charge was approaching a shadow-dim length of adobe buildings. But not unobserved. The Mexican cannons opened up from somewhere, belching out canister and solid shot. The air hummed gaudily, sections of earth fountained upward showering dirt. Mexican musketry blazed from windows, doors, from the flat-topped roofs and over adobe walls.

The Texans ran, they fell, their officers and NCOs were everywhere, their voices omnipresent, bawling orders.

"C'mon! Sound off! Let 'em know we're coming!"

The running Texans roared their war cries and the dawn air became a nightmare of wailing terror.

YeeeeeeYAH-wo-wo-wooo!

58

A long shallow ditch sprawled before them. They piled into it, jumping, sliding down, falling, then up again, and started firing over the earthen embankment. Tack got one shot off before a profane-mouthed sergeant—as fat and swollen as a grain sack belted about the middle—came charging along the prone line swishing the air with his sword and bellowing like an enraged bull.

"*Up! Up!* What're you stoppin' here for? This is a charge —*not a blame rest period!* C'mon! Git in them streets! Clean out them houses! *Up! Up 'n' forwaaard!*"

Tack scrambled out of the ditch and started running again, hearing in all the confusion of shouting and gun-slamming and war-crying, Rose's voice, yelling:

"Tack! Tack! Left! Turn left! Get behind that wagon!"

It was a two-wheeled old hayrack that was down to its knees in the rear. He dodged behind it and crouched as Mexican muskets went *wow wow* at him from over an adobe wall straight ahead. Rose came sliding in, dropped his shotgun and dug a grenade from his shirt, talking through his cigar-clenched teeth.

"Light one of 'em up! Show you how to clean out that patio!"

Tack got one of the bulky ironbound bombs out of his shirt, took a deep drag on his cigar, getting a good spark, and held it to the fore-shortened fuse.

"Pitch 'em out!" Rose cried.

The bombs hit the air, spinning in tight spirals, and dropped *whumph-whumph* inside the walled patio. A yellow flash and gray roar vacuum-packed the air, and Tack and Rose were on their feet again and running again, now into and through the voluminous coils of acrid smoke, and then into the shadow-drenched streets of Bexar.

The attack slowed, faltered, reorganized its cohesion and pressed onward. But slowly now, house to house and doorway to doorway. It was wicked work, sniper work. You scurried down mean little streets and dingy alleyways, with sniper bullets buzzing around your feet, and dodged into empty patios (you hoped) and through back doors into deserted houses (you prayed), and you pumped a load of buckshot into the shadowy rooms and crossed over to a window and ducked down and lit a bomb and lobbed it over into another window of another house, and then you went on.

But not all of you. . . .

Ben Milam led a run down a street toward the besieged Navarro House, and a Mexican sniper caught him cold with one clean shot from a rooftop. Milam went over backward into Sam Maverick's arms and he was dead before Maverick could lower him to the ground.

It went on for four days, hand to hand, house to house. It was a new kink in warfare.

Tack was sitting in a little shell-ruined patio in territory now firmly held by the Texans. He was having his lunch— not much, hardtack and canteen water. The slam-bang sound of the street fighting went on around him interminably, but he didn't pay any attention. He had grown callous to the noise.

A dust-daubed fellow of about Tack's age came through the gateway. He was attached to Tack's company but Tack didn't know him personally.

"Mind if I rest here a spell? My name's Richard Allen."

"Help yourself. I'm Tackett. Folks call me Tack."

Allen hunkered beside him with a heavy bone-weary sigh. When Tack offered him a bite of lunch he shook his head. He seemed almighty blue about something.

The rear door of the house facing them was open and there was a tangle of two-day-old dead men from both sides in there on the floor, fly-bothered.

"That sort of thing," Allen said nodding toward the dead, "is senseless. All of this killing is. Nobody really wanted this old house—except perhaps the family who once lived

60

here. And now that *we've* taken it we're not even keeping it."

"Well," Tack said, "nobody especially wanted Bunker Hill either. It's just one of those things that happen in war. Each little position along the way is a part of the larger and total picture. Battles aren't always fought over strategic positions."

"I see," Allen said sharply. "Then you're going to tell me that all the men who fought and died to get this one worthless house did it for a principle. Well, what *is* the principle behind a handful of us fighting all of Mexico? The Mexicans weren't invading our country. We don't own Texas. So why are we here dying for it?"

Tack stopped chewing and took a closer look at Allen. He recognized that peculiar I-don't-belong-here look in the youth's troubled eyes. It gave him an uneasy feeling, because he'd had doubts about the validity of his own presence in Texas.

"Say, what's eating you?" Tack asked gruffly.

Allen shrugged. "I simply don't believe in war, that's all."

"Well, what are you doing here then?"

"I belong here. I mean to say I'm a Texan—raised in Goliad. My dad believes in Texas independence—believes in it enough to die for it, I guess. When Austin marched against Bexar, Dad joined up. He insisted that I come, too. That's the way he is. He thinks I'm gutless and he's determined to make a man of me."

Tack didn't know what to say. He realized now that there was a marked difference between himself and Allen. Tack didn't like war for a very personal reason—*he* might get killed; but Allen was against war because of conviction.

"Well," he said finally, "I can't argue the right or wrong of war. All I know is it exists, always has. And when it comes and your country—"

"Don't wave flags at me, Tackett," Allen cut in. "That nonsense doesn't go with me."

No, it wasn't flags, Tack thought. It was more like the thought Hank had expressed . . . if one American has to fight anywhere in the world for his rights, then all Americans are tradition-bound to help him. Funny, he had scoffed at that sentiment once. Now he began to wonder. . . .

Right then a Lieutenant Tampas looked in at the gateway.

"Tackett, you and Allen are posted for my patrol tonight. We're going to make a recon on Old Bucket a Bombs."

Tack nearly dropped his lunch. "Bucket a Bombs?" he echoed.

It was a bad-news proposition. Next to the Alamo—where General Cós was making his last-ditch fight—the Bucket a Bombs was the only enemy stronghold left. It was a large sprawling public building and it had a proper name; however, due to the amount of firepower it had put forth during the past four days, the Texans had come to refer to it with sardonic affection as Old Bucket a Bombs.

It faced a broad stretch of fallow fields, which were closely surrounded by a depressed area of Mexican shanties, now deserted. Every time the Texans tried to take the place they found themselves caught in a crossfire of cleverly concealed cannons. Burleson's officers were confident that General Cós would give up the struggle once Old Bucket a Bombs was taken.

"That's what I said, Tackett," Lieutenant Tampas snapped.

He was like that—caustic, tough, easily ignited; the kind of man who believed that he had to do every dirty job by himself because he and only he was fully competent. He considered Tack lazy. He was convinced that Allen was chicken.

"There's going to be an attack against the stronghold tomorrow at dawn. Our job tonight is to locate those stinking Mex cannons."

Something unpleasant lurched in Tack's stomach.

"You mean we're supposed to knock those guns out?"

"No, Tackett. I didn't say that, did I? We're supposed to locate them. Then we report their positions, and our artillery—such as it is—goes to work and softens 'em up just before the attack." Tampas glanced at the silent Allen—a look loaded with scorn.

"See if you can rib up a little courage in that gutless wonder between now and midnight, Tackett. That's when we shove off. Twelve sharp. Think you'll be awake?"

Oh yes, Tack thought emptily. *Oh my yes. I'll be awake. Wide awake.*

6

THE PASSWORD WILL BE GUTS

The night was out of the vortex of bad dreams—nightmare-black and void of sound. Tack could just barely discern the vague outline of the Bucket a Bombs against the starless sky.

But of its hidden and deadly secrets he could see absolutely nothing: the sniper nests, the hidden cannons, the pit-and deadfalls which the Mexicans had concealed around their stronghold. These things had to be felt out. In the dark.

A frontier scout led the three-man patrol to the outer fringe of the Mexican shanties. Tampas talked to him for a minute, while Tack and Allen stood aside and shivered in the cold. They had nothing to say, didn't look at each other. Tack listened to what the scout was saying to the lieutenant.

"Right below this chere grade, you'll find thet the Mex shanties has been knocked all to heck 'n' gone by shellfire. The only bother you boys is liable to run into in thar is pit-

65

falls. Me 'n' some Arkansas boys has laid out some markers fer you. So folly 'em."

Pitfalls, Tack thought. That was nice—especially if they were the kind of widow-makers the swamp rats used to set along the Mississippi, back when river piracy was in bloom.

Allen seemed not to have heard. He was staring into the darkness toward the Bucket a Bombs.

I surely wish they hadn't picked him for this night crawl, Tack thought. *Or me either.*

"Then there's nothin' but a heap a shell holes in thet field till you come agin a ol' irrigation ditch which runs smack along the front a their position." The scout's voice was casual and nearly indifferent. He had a good thing going and he knew it. He led the sappy patrol to the scene of action—not too close—gave them directions, then turned around and went back to sit in the safety of the dark to wait for them to return . . . if they could.

Old veterans would say that the scout had a soft plank for himself, and he was busy nailing it down so that it couldn't get away.

Tack switched hands on his shotgun and reached to the back of his belt to see if the Elgin pistol was riding securely. He had borrowed it from Lou Rose. Allen had a carbine and Tampas carried a hunting knife and a North & Cheney pistol.

"Let's go," Tampas said to them.

He led the way into the silent ruins of the shanties, following the carefully arranged row of white markers which drew them along a narrow alleyway that was piled waist-high with black shards of wreckage. They were nearly clear of the shanties when an inquisitive rocket arched over the Bucket a Bombs.

It went up up up with a graceful serenity and seemed to select a spot for itself in the dark sky. It hovered there glowing brilliantly, shedding a weird rusty light over the ruins and fields.

"Down!" Tampas hissed, and he and Tack hit it together. *Now!*

But Allen reacted to inherent reflexes rather than to orders. When Tampas said "Down!" Allen leaped to the side of the alleyway and into the conglomeration of wreckage, seeking cover.

There was the sharp *crr-ack!* of weak boards giving way under pressure. Then a minor landslide of noise. Finally that hesitant pause that always exists between the death of sound and the triumph of silence. The rusty rocket dripped out sullenly.

Tampas began swearing—mean, whispered cuss words.

". . . that gutless wet-eared punk!" He crawled around Tack and over to the edge of the path, peered angrily into the black pit.

"Allen—Allen? You all right? Where are you?"

Allen's voice seemed to rise right from under them.

"Here. Down in some sort of pit or—something."

"Well, can you get out, man?"

A hesitation, then— "No. My left leg's caught in a bind."

"Judas," Tampas whispered dispiritedly. He started forward on hands and knees. Tack grabbed for his ankle.

"Wait a minute, sir. You might be crawling into a deadfall."

Like Tack's, Tampas' face was blackened with burnt cork, and all Tack could see of it were two pinpoint glints marking his eyes, and the wet gleam of teeth when Tampas spoke.

"What should I do about it, Tackett? Call for a rescue squad? That gutless wonder is part of my patrol. I'm responsible for him. You want me to order *you* to go in for him?"

Tack said nothing. He knew Tampas was only letting off steam. Tampas might not be the friendliest officer in the Texas army, but he never handed his dirty work to his men.

67

"So shut up and stay put," Tampas ordered. "If I'm caught in a deadfall, the patrol is all yours. Got that?"

Tack stared at the glinting eyes. Then he said, "Got it."

He stayed put on his belly, listening to Tampas scrambling around in the wreckage, praying, *Let them come out all right. Don't let me be left out here by myself. I honestly don't think I have the sand to crawl into that field all alone. . . .*

Something was coming out of the blackness toward him. It took on the round shape of a human head. For a second Tack looked into Allen's mute black face as the youth crawled by him. Then Tampas wormed out of the wreckage. Allen started to whisper.

"Thanks, Lieutenant. I couldn't have gotten out of there by—"

"Listen, bub," Tampas said in a quiet, furious voice. "You're one of those boys that come all apart when a bombshell goes over your head or when you accidentally see a couple of dead men. Right away you start whining, 'I object to war. I want to go home.' Well, maybe you'll finally talk yourself into deserting. I don't know or much care. But until you do—*you belong to me.* And when I give an order you better dang well obey it. Next time I say Down, you better start eating a hole in the earth. If you louse up this patrol by turning coward, I'll blast you in two."

"Sir," Allen began stiffly, "a man who conscientiously objects to war isn't necessarily a coward. Just because I believe that—"

"Did I give you permission to speak?" Tampas wanted to know. "Then hold it right there. All right, move out, both of you."

Nice friendly little group we are, Tack thought. He rose and moved out.

Don't wave flags at me, Allen had said. Well, maybe he was right. Maybe patriotism had gone out with the War of

1812. But if that was so, then what was Tack fighting for? What did Texas mean to him, personally? He didn't want to live there, and if he had no stake in the slab of ground that was under him, if he had no personal enmity for the Mexicans, then why was he crawling around out there 600 miles from home, risking his neck to inspect a couple of acres of fallow land that nobody wanted?

Out of my mind, he thought bitterly.

A sharp *ssst* of sound came back to him and he halted, going into a crouch, peering into the dark. It was Tampas calling his attention. Tack moved up.

Tampas was down on one knee. Directly in front of them lay the dark field. It stretched away, north and south, and faded into the pitchy gloom. Allen came in silently and hunkered next to them.

"Listen carefully," Tampas whispered. "We're going to break the patrol at this point. We'll each take fifty yards of dirt and crawl it. I'll take what's in front of us. Allen go left, Tackett right. Zigzag the entire section alloted you.

"If you come upon any kind of gun emplacement, get a fix on its position in your mind. The scout says there's an irrigation ditch running a few yards in front of the Bucket a Bombs. Also a ruin to the south of the ditch which used to be a hacienda. We'll meet between the two points in about half an hour."

He looked at Allen. "The password will be Guts," he said. "The counterword—Noguts."

Oh that really is nice, Tack thought angrily. *That will make Allen love him like a brother.*

"Just a suggestion, sir," Tack said. "I don't like the idea of splitting the patrol. It's too risky making contact later."

"Risky?" Tampas seemed to marvel at the word. "*O-oh my,* that would be *aw*-ful. The idea of us doing anything risky! Maybe you'd better take Allen's hand, Tackett. Maybe together the two of you can keep the nasty bogymans away. Now let's just shut up! We're splitting the

69

patrol. I don't want to be out here all night playing patty-cake patty-cake with dirt clods. Let's go."

Tack shrugged and moved into the field. He crawled into the ominous dark. Round black tumbleweeds stood delicately poised around him, waiting for a breeze to tumble them away. They spooked him. He kept thinking that Mexicans were hiding behind them.

There were shell holes, one two three four days old. He wormed around them, peering into their murky depths cautiously. Once he came upon the corpse of a dead Texan. . . . *Where did you come from, brother? What town in what state? Who did you leave behind?*

He paused, wondering about the time, and looked around for orientation. His visibility was limited to a few yards, but he could discern the dangerous bulk of the shanties on his right. He drew away from them, heading for the dark mass of the Bucket a Bombs.

He could tell from the way the shell holes met, merged and overlapped that he was in "live" ground—the sector where the Mexican guns cross-fired the field. A good place not to be in.

He was moving on his stomach, using elbows, gut muscles, knees and toes for locomotion. Two things were bothering him at this point: running into a guard post, and making contact with the rest of the patrol. The reunion was the touchy part about splitting a night crawl. Tack had to make himself known to another man when he wasn't absolutely certain that the other man was on *his* side.

It was a dandy way to catch a faceful of buckshot.

There were far fewer tumbleweeds now; yet each time he would approach one, the darn ball would suddenly bulge out of the gloom at him and an alarm bell would clang in his nervous system. Then he would whip up the shotgun and almost blast it.

Take it easy, he kept telling himself.

70

It was the unearthly silence that tormented him. It grew to the point where he became unreasonable about it. Why didn't someone *do* something? Anything to destroy the waiting suspense.

A huge mound of what looked like a rock pile formed on his right. The ruined hacienda. All right, that meant the ditch should be somewhere to his left. So—

Something moved in front of him. Nothing much, just a slight suggestion of motion. He put his head down, feeling the rasp of the pulverized dirt against his right ear. He waited, sensing that someone was right in front of him. He wasn't about to make the first overture and stop a bullet or a sword stroke in reply.

Whoever—whatever it was, was snaking closer. So close Tack could hear him. That meant the crawler was either very inexperienced or he had no idea that Tack was waiting for him. Tack's hand slid toward the trigger. And then a voice whispered:

"Guts?"

Tack felt like an old grease rag in the hands of a busy mechanic. He swallowed and murmured, "Noguts," thinking, *You can say that again.* Allen crawled up and they put their heads together.

"I think I've spotted Lieutenant Tampas," Allen said.

"*Think* you've spotted him? Don't you know?"

"No. There's someone five-six yards behind me, near the corner of the ruin. I got close enough to make out his form, but when I gave the word he wouldn't reply. It spooked me. So I crawled off."

Tack had that something's-gone-wrong feeling in his stomach. It was like a spearpoint of ice. But they couldn't resolve anything lying there in the dirt rubbing noses.

"All right," he whispered. "Lead me to him."

Allen squirmed about in a tight pivot and took off. Tack followed his boot soles. His senses were straining like fingers

71

reaching for something just beyond his grasp. The patrol had been bad from the beginning; now it was really sour. He felt inevitable violence hanging over him like a deadfall.

Allen stopped and Tack's head bumped his boots. Allen made a sign with his hand and Tack wormed alongside him and peered into the inky dark. After a wild moment of thinking he'd gone blind, he made out the dim bulge of a head. It was pointed toward them.

He barely breathed the word. *Guts?*

Nothing. Like talking to a wall. *Come on, Tackett, do something!* He drew the Elgin pistol and inched forward. He worked up to the prone figure, plowing a groove in the dirt with his chin. Then he looked. Then he set the pistol down and felt.

The spear that was in his stomach had reversed its direction. Now it was slicing into his heart. He wanted to stand up and walk away, wanted to say, I've had enough of this nightmare. It's time to wake up: not in this lousy place they call Texas, but in Mississippi where I belong. He rolled his head toward Allen.

"Dead," he whispered. "Tampas is dead."

Allen couldn't get it. He kept saying, "What? What do you mean? How dead? How can he be dead? What—"

"Shut up," Tack hissed urgently. "There's someone else out here in the field with us . . . a Mex crawling around with a knife."

He looked at the lieutenant. They'd never been friends. Tampas was hardheaded and tough and as bigoted as they come, but he'd been a good soldier. He got the job done.

That Mex must have laid still like a rut in the ground and let Tampas crawl right by him, Tack thought bleakly. And then wham in the back. He shivered, and raised his head, looking around.

The black mass of the Bucket a Bombs loomed threateningly over them. Dirt embankments had been thrown up all along the front to protect the doorways and lower windows.

72

The place gave him the jitters. It seemed to be watching them like a great dumb brute.

"Let's get away from here," he whispered. "Get in the cover of the ruin. We've got to decide what to do about those cannons."

"We'll never find them without the lieutenant." Allen sounded distracted. "It's hopeless out here in this pitch-dark."

Tack's nerve was ready to go four ways at once.

"Do what I tell you! I'm in charge now. Move out."

They went bread-and-butter around the dead man. Then Tack remembered Tampas' pistol and he lingered to search for it. But it was gone. *Lord*, he thought. *That Mex must have it.*

He was three yards behind Allen when he realized the fool had made another mistake. Allen was leading the way into the narrow slot between the rear of the hacienda and the embankment. Tack felt around for a dirt clod to peg at him. Too late. . . .

He heard the rough grind of wood moving against masonry, and a board or timber that Allen had unwittingly upset came down with a ringing *blam*!

Instantly rifle fire cut loose. Tack flattened out. He knew the riflemen were somewhere in the ruin, but they must have been well hidden. He couldn't see their flashes. They were firing on a set pattern, blindly raking the live ground before their position.

Then a crimson spark sizzled through the black air behind him and went *PLOW-MM*! And bits of stone, dirt and hot metal took off angrily, going everywhere. A grenade. A vacuum of expectant silence rushed in and swept up the night.

Will they call it quits now? Tack wondered.

They didn't. The riflemen started hammering fresh shots into the dark field. Then the Bucket a Bombs sprouted a questing flare into the sky and the night turned crimson.

73

Tack hugged the earth and it was like trying to press himself through a brick wall. Each grain of dirt under his face was red, and each grain cast its own eerie little shadow. *Oh go out,* he raged. *Go out!*

The flare faltered, then spluttered wanly downward. The blackness closed in again. The hidden rifles shut up. Good! Time to get out of there and . . .

Three flares went up from the Bucket a Bombs and splattered the sky, going *flam-flam-flamp.* Tack tilted his head and watched them. Green over green over green. That was that. The fat was in the fire. The Bucket a Bombs was signaling for cannon fire.

He couldn't crawl back into the field, and if he went into the ruins he might run smack into the riflemen. He started snaking toward the embankment, found a shell hole and slid in. A moment later a heavy gun somewhere in the old hacienda started to take the field apart, spewing canister with a vengeance.

Tack crouched in his hole and waited, the earth trembling and shaking beneath him. The explosions were like two hands clapping both his ears at once, and his eardrums were ringing on his brain. But he was all right. He was behind the hacienda and that meant he was in "dead" ground. It was just a matter of riding it out.

He waited, hugging the shotgun. Well, he had certainly discovered the location of one cannon!

It wasn't a shell hole. He realized that about the time the cannon fire petered out. He was evidently crouching in one end of that ditch Tampas had told them about.

He looked around, puzzled. It was too shallow for a defensive trench; and because of the way it abruptly began, he discounted the irrigation theory. Anyway, it was good cover. He decided to follow it, to see if it would get him away from the Bucket a Bombs.

He had gone about twenty yards when he realized the

74

ditch was deepening, turning into a trench. He could stand now. He leaned against the dirt wall, breathing short and quick, the way a man does when he's scared. He wished he knew if Allen were still alive; wished that *he* were someplace else. Anyplace.

He thought bitterly of the men he had seen lazying around on the Dillsburg porches. Where did they get off sitting and spitting their lives away while he was trembling in this foreign ditch? What sort of a deal was that? *Nuts,* he told himself. *You asked for this, so quit griping. Concentrate on staying alive.*

All right. Time to pick up the marbles that were left and get out of there. He'd had it for the night. His nerves were going to jelly and his brain seemed to be riding sidesaddle. He worked cautiously along the trench, his back to the wall, ready to open up with the shotgun on the first shadow that moved.

The trench took an abrupt right angle and continued on into the blackness. Tack hesitated indecisively at the corner. The turn led away from the Bucket a Bombs, aiming now for the live ground. It could be a sap, he thought, thrown out to an observation post or a gun emplacement. He didn't like that at all; but he didn't like the idea of going back either. He started down the trench.

"*Es un canalla,*" a quiet voice said.

Everything in Tack stalled at once and he seemed to be teetering witlessly on the brink of an abyss. He couldn't breathe, couldn't think. It was so black in the trench that he had almost blundered right into the enemy. He was practically among them!

He quickly quelled his panic and harassed his wits into alignment. The voice had spoken just ahead of him. He reached down. There were three dirt steps under his hand. Probably led up to a shallow dugout. The second gun emplacement! He eased his head over the rim and watched the vague shadows until they moved.

The squatty and stationary shape of the gun, straight ahead . . . gunner to the left, his back to Tack . . . swab man on the right, also with his back to Tack. Anyone else?

"*Ya lo creo*," another voice muttered.

Heyday! That one was sitting smack on Tack's right ear. Must be the loader. Tack pulled back and bit at his lower lip. If he had one of Lou Rose's grenades, and if there were some way of lighting the blame thing without the whole world seeing him do it, he could just lob it up there among them and throw himself to the bottom of the trench. Well, that was out. . . .

His hand tightened on the shotgun. If they were just bunched together it would be all right. One double-barreled blast. But they were scattered. He didn't know what to do. What *could* he do all by himself? Anyhow, why should he stick his neck out?

Go on, Tackett, creep out of here. Go on back and report you've located the other cannon . . .

But they might shift it, and the one in the hacienda too, now that they've used them tonight . . .

But it doesn't really matter, does it? It's not your responsibility. All you were supposed to do was locate them. Yeah . . .

But still—I might get lucky. I could take the loader with the right barrel, and maybe catch the other two with the left. Yeah.

It wasn't so tough when you thought about it. It was just that initial step that was bad. *All right. Rib yourself up to it.* But he couldn't seem to start. That first step was a monster.

"*Café*." A whispered voice came from somewhere behind him.

"*Solo*," the loader above Tack hissed.

Tack couldn't believe it. Word and counterword. The Mexican crawler with the knife was coming back in. Coming into the trench behind him. He was caught in the middle!

77

But there was no question about taking that initial step now.

I'll take the emplacement first. For just a second the crawler will think it's them firing. Right barrel for the loader, left for the gunner and swabber, then the Elgin for the crawler. If I can get it out in time. If if. All right. ALL RIGHT. Start it! In another second that crawler will be on your back.

He sucked air, stepped onto the first step and swung the shotgun up. The silhouette of the loader hulked toward him, saying, *"Quién es?"*

The right barrel kicked *KA-BLOWM*! and Tack saw the loader spin away in the flash. Then he swept the muzzles around just as the gunner and the swabber turned, and he lighted the emplacement with a quick bright flash from the left barrel, and saw the gunner topple, and knew in that instant that they had been too far apart and that he had missed the swabber completely.

A sword blade glinted in the swabber's black hand and he rushed Tack with a half-strangled cry as Tack reversed the shotgun in his hands and swept the butt up under the Mexican's oncoming chin. And that took care of him.

Behind you! his brain roared, and he swung completely around to face the crawler, dropping the shotgun and clawing for the Elgin pistol. But he spun too fast and his boot slipped on the dirt step, shot out, and he came down hard on his tailbone, sprawling in the gun emplacement's mouth.

The crawler's gun went *POW* right over Tack's head and the stabbing flame tossed a flicker of light in the center of the trench and smeared the dirt walls a rusty color, and for a split second Tack saw just where the Mexican was and the Elgin pistol jumped in his hand as he yelled, "That's for Tampas!"

The Bucket a Bombs whacked out another flare, but before it could finish its climb into the sky, there was a terrific explosion as the old ruined hacienda across the field seemed to come apart at the seams in a great blare of light.

Tack crouched as a wave of compressed air whooshed over him. He couldn't imagine what on earth had happened and he didn't have any time to waste wondering about it. He spiked the cannon with a pistol ramrod and, just in case that didn't do the trick, he tossed half a dozen handfuls of dirt down the muzzle. That would blow the barrel to shreds the first time the Mexicans tried to use it.

The Bucket a Bombs was crackling with musket fire and shouting questions in the dark. After a while they shut up and the great shapeless building returned to its black brooding.

Time for Tack to ramble—before they sent some Mexican scouts out to see what was doing in the hacienda and the gun emplacement. He crawled over the embankment and into the live ground. Another night like this and the Texans would have to send him home strapped in a wet sheet, the way mental patients were treated. Too bad he had to leave Tampas' body out there, and probably Allen's as well. Too bad about a lot of things, he thought.

Allen was waiting for him with the frontier scout, on the rise beyond the shanties.

Tack said, "I thought you were dead!"

"I crawled into that beat-up old hacienda when the cannon fire started," Allen told him.

"Into the hacienda? Didn't you know there were riflemen in there?"

"Not till I got inside. I could hear 'em banging away from up on a platform in an angle of the wall. That's where they had that cannon." Allen paused. He seemed a little embarrassed. "They were so busy they didn't even know I was there. I found a big pile of their powder charges right under the platform. So I crawled back down an alleyway and got under cover . . . then I fired my gun into their powder."

Tack looked at him blankly.

"*You* blew up the hacienda?"

Allen raised his head and nodded with resolution.

"Yes, I did. I was hiding under them, listening to them bang away on that damn cannon of theirs, and I kept thinking about the lieutenant. He didn't like me, but he climbed down in that hole to dig me out. That cost him about five minutes. Maybe if I hadn't taken those five minutes from him, he'd have missed that Mexican with the knife. Maybe he'd still be alive. So—the more I thought about it, the more I realized I owed him something. So I stopped that cannon the only way I could."

Tack nodded, remembering what he had unconsciously yelled when he shot the Mexican crawler—*That's for Tampas*. Perhaps they had both started to discover a part of the reason for why they were fighting in Texas. . . .

The Bucket a Bombs was carried by the Texans at dawn.

At 6:30 A.M. General Cós threw in his hand. The Mexican army pulled back over the Rio Grande under parole. The battle for Bexar was over.

7

I NEED TWO VOLUNTEERS

The Alamo was a great sprawling affair covering three barren acres. The main part was a bare rectangular compound the size of a city block. It was called the Plaza and it was hemmed in by adobe huts and stone walls. The walls were twelve feet high.

Cós had done very little toward fortifying the place. The west side contained the officers' quarters and headquarters. The south end was ribbed with the "low barracks" and the main gate. The north end consisted of a long firing platform and a few huts. The east side held the "long barracks" and the hospital; the east was also backed up by two large, walled corals. There was a noticeable gap between the east side and the south end. This gap was the chapel yard, which faced the blocky-looking Alamo church.

It was a ruinous old building with walls four feet thick and practically no roof at all. The sacristy was arched, but Cós had built up an earth ramp almost the entire length of the nave, to house a gun platform.

Yet it was the very age and neglected condition of the place that seemed to lend the Alamo its mystic air. It was so deliberately uncared for and remote that it had about it the suggestion of a primordial beast crawling off by itself to die in splendid isolation and independence. Yet it was destined never to die.

Tack noticed this odd emanation of nameless enchantment the moment he and Hank entered the compound and looked silently around at the Plaza and its mute hutments. It seemed to take hold of you like a traumatic memory; you might in time forget its particular details, but you would never forget the place as a whole.

Bexar was still in the throes of a victory celebration, and Tack and Hank—tired of the endless yelling and pistol shooting and horse racing—had slipped off by themselves to inspect the Alamo.

Most of the army figured the war was over. Even General Burleson had gone home to his family, leaving the command in a Colonel Johnson's restless hands. But some, like Hank, believed it was only the beginning.

"We've only licked Cós," he said. "Not Santa Anna."

"Yes, but most of the Texans say Santa Anna is nothing but a comic-opera general," Tack said. "They figure he's about as much threat as a lame gopher."

"Then they don't know much about buffoons who set themselves up as dictators. They are the most dangerous of all. Their melodramatic and clownish minds drive them to do things that a reasonable man would never dream of attempting. You wait and see. Santa Anna is the type of man who has to prove to the world—*not* to himself—that he is important."

Tack spotted a lone slim figure standing on the long barracks roof. The man raised his hand in the pale Christmas sun and waved. Tack and Hank walked over to the east ladder to meet him.

He was a very dapper, handsome man in dark clothes,

about thirty. He reminded Tack of the Black Knight in Ivanhoe. There was something Gothic in his manner.

"My name is James Bonham," he said quietly, smiling.

Tack had heard of him. He was a lawyer from the Carolinas. He had arrived with the volunteers known as the Mobile Greys three days after the fall of Bexar. His was a rebellious nature—the type of man that Texans would always welcome wholeheartedly.

He had been expelled from South Carolina College at seventeen, for demonstrating against the food. He had been involved in the stormy Nullification Crisis at twenty-three, as a soldier. When he was twenty-four he caned a brother lawyer for insulting a lady, and when the judge jumped on him and ordered an apology, Bonham had offered to pull the judge's nose instead. He got ninety days.

Disappointed in love at twenty-seven, Bonham had shifted to Alabama, then on to Mobile in 1835, in time to become a part of the vortex of the Texas storm. Mobile had sent him to Sam Houston as their courier of goodwill. Now he was a lieutenant in the Texas cavalry and under Colonel James Bowie's orders.

"Have you noticed it?" he asked Tack and Hank.

"Noticed what?" Hank asked.

"The grasp of this place," Bonham said, looking at the empty rooms and silent walls. "It has a draw to it. It gets invisible hooks into you and won't let go. As if it were ghost-ridden."

Hank smiled. "Yes, I have. But I think it must be like any historic landmark. And I imagine it only works when you are alone in it. The spell would be broken with a multitude around."

"I wonder," Bonham murmured.

A group of officers came through the gate making all the vocal sounds indicative of an argument. Tack recognized Colonel Neill, second in command of the Bexar army.

"I've never heard anything so absurd in my life!" Colonel

Neill cried in obvious vexation. "This idiot Doctor Grant proposes to carry the war into Mexico *without any authorization at all!* And now he has most of the army convinced that if they cross the Rio Grande and take the port of Matamoros, they'll come home with more treasure than Cortés stole from the Aztecs!"

"Well," a lawyer-engineer named Green Jameson said, "perhaps Matamoros *is* loaded with booty."

"Booty!" Neill cried. "It's loaded with fleas and flies and lizards. I've been there. You want to know the real reason Dr. Grant has dreamed up this expedition? He owns land down there, and it would benefit him to liberate it from the Mexicans! And now he's convinced that fool Colonel Johnson that *he* should go, too!"

"Let's hear more of this," Bonham suggested. He and Tack and Hank drifted toward the vociferous group of officers.

The meat of the matter was this: Dr. Grant, a mighty shrewd Scot, had convinced Colonel Johnson and 200 volunteers that they should march to Matamoros and pick gold nuggets off the streets. Johnson was so starry-eyed about the plan that he had turned the Bexar army over to Neill and had ripped off to get the provisional governor's permission.

But Grant couldn't wait for him. Now, on the last day of 1835, he and the 200 treasure hunters were marching off to Matamoros with everything they could get their hands on— money, saddles, arms, food, blankets, medical supplies, and horses. Neill was left with exactly 104 men to defend Bexar. And come January, twenty-four of these volunteers would decamp for home.

"How in the Lord Harry's name am I to hold Bexar with eighty underfed, partially armed men?" Neill cried.

"Forget Bexar," Bonham interposed. "Concentrate your forces here in the Alamo."

Neill looked around at the great spread of rambling walls and shook his head in despair.

"Well, we can only try," he said. "But eighty men will never be able to hold a place this size."

"Perhaps Santa Anna will back down," Jameson said doubtfully. "Maybe he won't march against us after all."

Neill grunted. "Don't you believe it. He'll be here all right. The question is: when?" He looked at Tack and Hank. "I need two volunteers."

Tack balked. He'd been in the army just long enough (and around Lou Rose) to learn that you never never volunteered for anything. But Hank stepped forward and said "Yes, sir," promptly. So what could Tack do—make like a scared rabbit? He came to attention.

"One man to go down the Laredo Road," the colonel said. "The other to follow the Presidio Road. If I am to hold this outpost, I must have eyes! I must know what Santa Anna is up to. Whether he is advancing, or if he has stopped indefinitely in San Luis Potosí as rumor says. You will each take a horse and proceed south until you contact his army. The moment you encounter the Mexicans, ride back here in all haste." He paused and studied them for a moment under his shaggy brows.

"You are both very young," he said in a tired voice, "and probably very idealistic. That's why you haven't run off with those older treasure-happy fools to Matamoros, or left for home like all those idiots who think a war is won with just one victory. I thank you both for holding on—in the name of liberty."

Tack cleared his throat. He felt sort of low and mean because he had momentarily balked when Hank had not.

What's wrong with me? he wondered. *What am I afraid of? All I have to do is ride down the road a bit and maybe get a peek at Santa Anna's army, and then ride for home. Nothing really dangerous about that, is there?*

"That's all right, Colonel," he said impulsively. "We're glad to scout for you."

At that moment he really meant it.

85

Tack's innate caution sent him to the printer's shop in Bexar.

The shop's windows had been shattered during the battle, and now they were boarded over and the printer worked by whale-oil lanterns, even during the daylight hours.

There was a stubby-built old-timer lounging around in there, squirting tobacco juice through the door as if it were no feat at all to spit four yards. He was buckskin-clad and had a mangy-looking beard like a mare's nest. One of his eyes was missing. But the remaining orb seemed to miss nothing at all.

Tack handed the printer a slip of paper.

"Can you make me up some cards to read like this?"

The printer snuffed his left nostril and took the paper into the light, reading aloud: "Francis B. Tackett. Representative Journalist for the Ohio Whig Newspaper."

The old-timer winked his only eye at Tack.

"Francis. Thet's a gal's name, hain't it?"

"It was my mom's idea," Tack explained. "Don't blame me. That's why I go by the name of Tack."

The old-timer centered his attention on a fly droning just above the doorsill and hit the luckless insect with a well-aimed splat.

"I'm Tom Hendricks," he mentioned. "My daddy was *the* Captain Hendricks thet marched agin Quebec with Benedict Arnold." Then he glared at Tack with his good eye, as if defying him to say "Never heard of him," or to say a word against General Arnold.

But Tack was up on his history, and he was one of those (and there were many in his time) who still realized that Benedict Arnold was the best general in the Revolutionary War.

"I'm glad to meet you. Where I come from, folks say Arnold's march was the greatest march in history."

Old Tom masticated his chaw in delighted embarrassment.

"I'm almighty glad you should think so, boy," he said, beaming. "Because I'm liable to go to scratch whenever I hear some fool talk agin Gen'ril Arnold."

"Benedict Arnold was a traitor," the printer commented as he set type in his tray. "Ever' American knows that."

Old Tom's eye blinked rapidly and he spat a few amber drops into his horny palms and worked them together vigorously. Then he started to climb over the counter. Tack grabbed him.

"Hold on! He's got a right to his opinion, hasn't he? It's a free country, isn't it? Free speech, free press, all of that."

Old Tom thought about it, eyeing the printer furiously.

"Wall, I suppose hit is. But ifn he goes to say hit agin, I'll purely turn him tail-end to! Insultin' Arnold is the same as insultin' my daddy! You hear me, you inky-faced type-setter?"

The printer took an appraising look at the rangy leather-faced old man, and nodded. "All right," he muttered.

Tack was also taking an appraising look at the old-timer.

"Are you a Texan, Tom?"

"I reckon. Ifn two years outn a man's sixty years makes him a Texan. Cause thet's how long I been down here. And from the way I feel about all this space 'n' freedom, I 'spect I'll die here."

"How would you like to go out on a scout with me for the Texas army?" Tack asked.

Old Tom studied him with a contemplative eye.

"Whar you from, boy? I'm partic'lar who I team up with."

"Texas," Tack said promptly. "If one month out of a man's eighteen years makes him a Texan."

"Done!" Tom said, and he put out his hand. "I'm always powerful pleased to meet up with a brother Texan!"

87

8

THEY'RE ALL AROUND US!

The mountain stood up from the prairie. Straight up, from the shoulders of the pines, like a sentinel post of granite, watching with godlike tolerance from its castle crags and turret peaks the dismal and dreary march of oncoming winter. Lord of the rolling lands of greasewood and cacti and the thousands of candlelike yuccas and the great carpets of golden brittlebush flowing over the slopes and benches of the upper levels, the mountain remained a brooding deity—remote yet very near.

An iron-ribbed wind led the way across the plains, stampeding a huge herd of rolling tumbleweeds. The sky was a turquoise weather breeder going on around without a hitch, not a trace of clouds. Old Tom studied it with his contemplative eye.

"We're in for some more wet. Snow, too, when we git up above."

Tack was a believer. Wars, it seemed, always had to be

fought in wet weather—Lord knows why. That was history's rule.

They were riding through a gusty wonderland. Far ahead a great dark sea of tall grass undulated in a milk-cold breeze. Peaceful, quiet . . .

Tack heard a Sonora pigeon voice his liquid call from the top of a lone sahuaro, and a gambrel partridge waddled out of a mescal shelter to see what all the fuss was about. Once they passed a dun-colored abode, its wide porch overrun with vines. There was a bit of untended flower garden, and beyond that stood a rude barn built on the Indian order —sahuaro poles and mud, with a small corra made of thorny ocotillo.

The farm wife came out and looked at them, and Tack touched the brim of his hat. *"Buenas tardes, señora,"* he called.

"Vaya con Dios, caballeros," she said to them.

I hope so, Tack thought.

They had been riding south for days, following the Presidio Road when there was a road to follow, more often trusting to Tom's infallible sense of direction. He was a handy man in a wilderness. He had prairie know-how. He was also a fund of information.

"Anybody thet don't think old Santy Anny won't fight jest 'cause he acts like a crazy clown, is a shore-dab fool! That old Anny's as wily and mean as a mink. Mebbe you don't know how the mink works? Most folks look at him and think My, ain't he elegant in his handsome coat a hair! Huh! They don't know Mr. Mink. He's as cruel as a Apache, vicious as a wolverine. He can out-endure a mule and he's as wary as a shedding rattler. He can travel hull miles a distance and show up whar nobody ever expects him to."

Tom spat to the left, then he went on. "A mink will go into a duckpond in broad daylight and clown about like a kitten fer hours, see? And all the ducks will float around and gawk at him in wonderment. Then at night Mr. Mink will slip back to the pond and cut the throat of ever' last one a them fool ducks. Thet's Santy Anny. Thet's how he works, how he got control a Mexico. Tricks like thet."

But it all seemed far away to Tack right then, remote, belonging to the undefined future. He didn't want to think of Santa Anna and the war. His mind was lazily on the face of the vast raw land sprawling endlessly around him . . . which only shows how helpless a man can be when he is removed from his own element.

But Tom—though he was yammering away about minks and Mexican generals—had his senses closely attuned to the mesa, and all at once his head went up and his bright eye swept from right to left, and he whispered:

"Turn toward them west hills, quick!"

Tack blinked. "What?"

"*Ride!* You blame fool!"

Tom palm-slapped the rump of Tack's mare and the horse went off in a bolt, backrolling her eyes. Tack looked around in startled bewilderment . . . but not for long.

"*OW! OW! OW!*" A gang of mounted Comanches came right out of the gorse-covered earth and charged toward the two white men.

Tack hunched over and booted in his spurs. "*Hee-YAH!*" he yelled, and that big driving-shouldered mare laid back her ears and went charging over ground that was so hard that Tack could feel the cutting, pounding jar of the chopping hoofs up his spine and into his neck and under the roof of his skull—heading now for the scarlet glory of the ocotillos crowding along the hillside.

Old Tom was thundering up on his left, his crooked pipe-stem arms flapping at his sides like a gaunt crow working up enough pressure to take off, and those Comanches—who were considered the best horsemen in America—were boiling along in their chip-flying red-dust wake and gaining, slow, sure, steady.

90

Then the rocky pass of an old dried river bed shot open before Tack and he and the mare went swerving into it with the red and salmon and orange and pink of the chollas and opuntias sweeping by in a brilliant smear of color, and they went banging down the broad wash of white gravel in the old arroyo bed, the hoofs clacking furiously over the stones, and burst into the open again and found themselves in a fat plot of bunch grass which aproned a guzzle of water.

Beyond the creek sat the old burnt-over remains of a homestead. Nothing had been left standing except a roofless stone springhouse.

They piled across the creek in a great thrash of hoof-splashed water, and up the bank, Tack and the mare both leaning against the gravitation rise, and now the hoofs leaving large U prints behind in the mud, and then they were charging into the grass-thickened yard and he heard the *sss-wit sss-wit* of arrows going by.

Tom yelled and went down in a great flurry of grass and flying mane and pawing hoofs, and Tack looked back and swung the mare's head around and reined in.

Tom was already on his knees and clutching his rifle in his right hand, but an arrow was sticking through his left arm.

"Ride, Tack! I'll hold 'em from the springhouse!"

"No!" Tack jumped from the foaming mare and swung his shotgun barrel at her rump. "*S'git*, girl!" He ran toward his friend.

A startled yelp sounded from somewhere beyond the creek, followed by the crack of a musket. Tom looked at his thrashing horse. "Fore right shank broke," he said, raising his rifle.

Tack didn't watch him put the animal out of its misery; he was looking for Indians and didn't have far to look. A brave on a pony was crashing across the creek, shooting silver sparks of water as he came. He gained the shelving

bank, urging the pony on with a bucking rhythm of his naked body. He swerved the nag, cutting obliquely for Tack, raising a feathered spear as he came.

Tack dropped to his knees—the pony and its painted rider looming larger, larger—and threw up his shotgun. The pony seemed to be right on top of the gunsight and the Comanche's *EEE-YAAAH*! threw Tack's equilibrium into a ringing glassy ball of shock.

He pulled the right trigger and the Indian went over backward as the war pony veered sharply away from the two crouching men and the dead horse in the grassy yard. Tack shoved up and got Tom on his feet and they started running. Out of the corner of his eye Tack saw other gaudy horsemen splashing across the creek, coming good-gosh along to cut them off from the springhouse.

Tack gave the lurching Tom a shove through the doorway and swung around with the shotgun. The left barrel went *KA-BLAM*! Then he darted through the doorway. He looked around quickly. The interior of the springhouse was small and square, the unroofed walls barely five feet high. There was a circular well opening in the center of the floorboards, and an unused stack of warped boards along the north wall—probably intended for the roof.

Tack divided the boards in half, taking one stack over to the south wall. Now he had two makeshift firing platforms. He gave Tom the shotgun to load and took the old-timer's 5-shot .44 pistol, checked the caps, and stepped up on the boards and looked over the north wall. The creek ran away along his right; on his left and at the corner of the springhouse stood a straggly thicket of smokebushes. The bunch grass crowded up all around like a hungry sea.

The Comanches were riding parallel to the north wall, firing as they went. He opened up on them with the pistol, holding his wrist in his left hand, panning the barrel. Out of four shots he hit one of them. He stepped down, calling to Tom.

"Here, reload the pistol. I'm down to one shot."

He took the shotgun and trotted around the well opening to the south-wall firing step. Two braves were starting to ford the creek, and he knocked one of them into the water with the first shot. The other one swung his nag's head around and got out of there, riding low.

A furious volley of bullets whapped along the wall, but it was only a vindictive outburst. The Comanches had pulled back. Tack went over to Tom to take care of his wound.

"Notch hit with your knife, then break hit off, Tack." Tom gritted the words through his teeth. "Pull the rest out through the hole. Quick! Ain't got all day. Thet arrerhead's pizon."

"Poison?" Tack gasped.

"Yep. Trick they larn from the Chiricahuas. They put

rattlers in willow baskets, then tease the snakes by pokin'
arrers through the basket. The rattler strikes at the arrerhead and the venom dries on hit. Soon's it hits somethin'
wet—like a man's blood—it starts to work. *Uagh!* Smarts
some. All righty, now gather up some splinters 'n' mesquite
roots and make a fire."

Tack did as directed, frantic at the thought that Tom
might suddenly keel over dead. He got a little cup-sized fire
going, and Tom said, "Take off one a your spurs and heat
up one a the rowels. Then ream out these two holes in me
with hit."

Lordy! Tack thought. But he did it, had to, getting the
long rowel red-hot and sinking it into the puffy, raw wound,
first front, then back, and shuddering as the hot blunt metal
sizzled angrily. Tom's only concession to the pain was a
single grunt.

Heyday, Tack thought, *I wish I had this old man's
strength.*

The afternoon sun began westing for the low, close-in
hills. The Comanches had settled down to a sniping siege,
trying at the same time to sneak closer and closer to the
encircled springhouse. Tack, shifting from south wall to
doorway to north wall, had to keep expending his ammunition to hold them back. He was running powerful low on
powder and ball.

Once, during a long lull, he stepped down to the opening
in the floor and hand-cupped water to his mouth the way an
Indian does, watching through the doorway as he drank. He
winked at Tom. The old-timer looked ashen and sick in the
twilight.

"We'll hold out, eh, Tom?" he said encouragingly. "Arnold and your dad had it worse than this at Quebec."

"Sure," old Tom said hoarsely. "Much worse."

But right at that moment neither of them really believed it.

The twilight was turning dull pink; soon it would be gray. The lull in the fighting seemed inordinately long.

"Watch 'em, Tack," Tom said. "This is the bad time. If they're going to do something, then it'll be—"

And it was. There was the sudden gut-grabbing savage scream, and a dozen mounted Comanches came boiling around either corner of the burned-down homestead; converged in the center of the yard like a blown froth and swept on in a swift drumming rush, the bobbing weeds hissing under the horses, and the hoofs pounding like logs and stones tumbling over and over in a flood.

"They're rushing the doorway," Tack yelled.

He fired, fired, feeling the quick spastic jolt of the hot shotgun in his hands and shoulder, and passed it back to Tom to reload, and brought up the .44, praying, *Make 'em stop! Please God, make 'em stop!*

The charge turned into a struggling pandemonium. Horses and braves went down rolling, sprawling, bouncing; most of them turned away, humping over, yip-yipping as they rode off, their high yelping thin and piercing and flung ahead.

Three of them would never run again. Tack followed a brave running on foot toward the smokebush thicket with the .44 barrel, and pulled the trigger.

The .44 said *click.*

He couldn't believe it. He jerked the trigger again. Same result. He turned and looked at Tom in the gathering dusk. Tom shook his head and threw the shotgun aside.

"Thet does hit, Tacky. Spang out of ammo."

A cannonball of apprehensive horror started rolling over and over in Tack's stomach as he reached for his knife.

"They're in the smokebushes, in the grass," he whispered. "They're all around us!"

Old Tom nodded and reached into the fire for a burning stick. "Just whar I want 'em," he muttered. He raised the flame-licked stick and stepped up on the boards with Tack and pegged the firebrand far into the smokebush thicket.

"Throw 'em out, boy! This whole blame homestead's a tinderbox!"

Wildly, Tack and Tom lobbed one burning stick after another into the thicket and surrounding bunch grass. A finger of flame wiggled through the smokebush, caught with a crackle of sparks and shot up into a tongue of fire. Then the bunch grass took hold and the twilight breeze off the hills fanned it into a beautiful whamping carpet of flame.

The fire spread, spread, the smoke rolling away into the dusk like the white hunchback of a land-bound wave. All around the homestead Comanches sprang from cover with startled yelps and went pelting off toward the arroyo.

Tom cackled excitedly. "Them redsticks will never larn how dangerous hit is to corner a wounded old grizzly bar like me!"

Tack could have hugged the old-timer.

A smoke-hazy starlit night was standing over them when they heard the clop-clop of hoofs and the jingle-jank of a mounted troop cantering up to the twice-scorched old homestead.

"*Alto!*" a voice called in Spanish. Halt! A moment later a tall dragoon officer in a moon-glinting breastplate came striding across the smoldering yard toward the springhouse.

"*Quién es?*" he asked as he approached. "Who are you? We saw your fire from the road. I am Lieutenant José María Torres of General Antonio López de Santa Anna's army."

"Out of the fire into the blame fryin' pan," Tom muttered, sagging in Tack's arms.

9

I ATTACK! I BURN! I KILL! I WIN!

General Antonio López de Santa Anna looked like a misplaced holdover from the Napoleonic wars. He was short, stout, almost forty. His hair was curly and black and combed forward in the Caesar and Bonaparte manner. His uniform was a brilliant color scheme, purple encrusted with gold braid and frogged with silver. He wore so many medals on his chest Tack thought he would topple over from the sheer weight of them whenever he stood up.

The general's bedizened collar was so high and stiff that he had to turn his upper body in order to turn his head. His military hat was a great fore-and-aft job, decked over with frothy plumes. It looked as though he were wearing a rowboat full of colored soapsuds. His face was deceptive. It looked pleasant.

He received Tack and Tom and Lieutenant Torres in his striped marquee on the road between Monclova and Saltillo. It was dawn, January 22, 1836. Santa Anna had been seven weeks marching from Mexico City.

"Well? Well?" he snapped irritably at Lieutenant Torres. "Why am I bothered at this unholy hour?"

"General, these two *Norte Americanos* were attacked by Comanches. My advance guard saw their fire and rode to their assistance. We took twelve Indian prisoners, Excellency."

"Mother and father and all the in-laws of Judas!" Santa Anna cried. "What do I want with Comanche prisoners? Shoot them!"

Torres looked slightly stunned.

"Pardon, Excellency. Perhaps I did not make myself clear. The Indians surrendered when we boxed them in an arroyo. I consider them prisoners of war."

Santa Anna couldn't believe such insubordination.

"*You* consider them! You! *Un canalla*—a dumbbell? John and Peter Moses, *I* do all the considering here! What can you do with Comanches, eh? Nothing! You can't make soldiers of them: they are too savage. If we keep them we must post valuable men to guard them, *si*? We must give them our food, *si*? *Nombre d'un nombre*, have I wasted all my years trying to teach you fools to be officers? How many times must I explain to you the only way to make war is to attack! Burn! Kill!"

Tack wet his lips. He had no love for the Comanches, but he thought along the same lines as Lieutenant Torres: a prisoner was a prisoner, not something you shot like a wild dog. He realized that he had never before met anyone whom he wholeheartedly hated—until this moment. He looked around the huge tent with distaste.

Santa Anna's equipage included monogrammed china, crystal decanters, racks of overly gaudy uniforms, a painting depicting Napoleon brooding over a tangled battlefield of wounded and dying French soldiers watching him with pain-glazed adoring eyes, and a silver chamber pot.

"Now that we have disposed of the Comanche question,"

Santa Anna said briskly, "what of these two?" He nodded at Tack and Tom. "Why haven't they been shot?"

"Shot, your excellence?" Torres asked hesitantly.

"By the mangy beard of Jonah! What else? They're *Norte Americanos*, aren't they? We are at war with them, eh? What did you think we would do with our enemies—slap them on the wrist and send them home? I have come to teach them a lesson! I have come to drive them out of Texas once and for all! To annihilate them!"

"We're not here as Texas soldiers, General," Tack said. It was obvious that he would have to resort to a ruse in dealing with this ambitious madman. He produced one of his fake cards.

"I'm from a newspaper. And Tom here is my guide."

Santa Anna sniffed suspiciously as he studied the card.

"Aren't you rather young to be a newspaperman?" he asked.

"Well, sir," Tack replied promptly, "as to that—aren't you rather young to be the president of an entire nation?"

Santa Anna was pleased with this reply. He somehow managed the awkward task of seeming to strut while standing still. He took a moment to preen the epaulets on his shoulders: each one as large as a chopping board and cascading great drippings of silver braid.

"Well! And why have you come to Mexico uh—Señor Tackett?"

"To report on the war, General."

"Insurrection!" Santa Anna corrected him. "An open rebellion led by a handful of ingrates who will very shortly be taught the folly of complaining against the just and benevolent laws of Antonio López de Santa Anna!"

Tack started toward the general's field desk.

"May I use your quill and paper, General? I would like to quote that astounding statement while it's fresh in my mind."

Santa Anna cleared his throat and beamed with self-importance.

"*Ciertamente, ciertamente*—certainly, certainly. And what of your guide? He looks ill. Does he need medical attention?"

Tack figured he had the general pegged. The man was so puffed up with ego that you could lead him like a horse wearing blinders, with one or two flattering words.

"He was wounded with a poisoned arrow, General. I never would have been able to make my report to the rest of the world regarding your grand army without his assistance."

"*Nombre de Nombre*, Torres!" Santa Anna exploded. "Why do you just stand there like a fence post? Can't you see this good man needs a doctor? By the rope that hung Judas, must I take care of everything myself!"

Alone with Santa Anna, Tack helped himself to a camp-stool and prepared to make notes.

"Your army is how strong, General?"

Santa Anna strutted to and fro before his desk, one hand stuck inside the front of his jacket in the Napoleon way.

"Some 4,000 men and twelve cannon, 400 cavalry, 80 wagons, 400 mules, 3,000 muleloads of flour, 300 *fanegas* of biscuit, and two mortars."

Heyday! All of this against eighty Texans in Bexar! Tack jotted down the figures, and asked:

"And your plans regarding San Antonio de Bexar?"

"Annihilation!" Santa Anna said sharply. "Bexar is the cornerstone of this insurrection. It must be reduced to ashes. All its defenders must be eliminated out of hand!"

"You mean to say you won't consider a capitulation?"

"Exactly that!" Santa Anna stated. Then he turned and looked at Tack, and for just a moment Tack saw the man who was doomed forever to hide under the clown's façade —not the soldier or the dictator, but the helplessly ambition-driven man.

"I have no choice, señor. America means to take the territory of Texas from my country. If I am to stop this acquisition, I must act in a manner so sharp, so startling, that Americans will never again attempt to encroach on Mexico."

Tack knew it would be futile to remind the general that Mexico had invited the Americans into Texas, had practically handed them the territory on a silver platter. Instead he said:

"But surely so sharp a measure as total annihilation can only create hatred. And hatred breeds retribution."

"American retribution doesn't mean *that* to me!" Santa Anna was the great general once again. "I am a student of Napoleon, you know. The greatest general of them all! I attack! I burn! I kill! I win! Nothing else matters."

Tack stared at the floor, thinking, *But Napoleon died an obscure death on an obscure island. And he left France in ruins.*

Leaving the marquee Tack was not too surprised to see an infantry sergeant fall in behind him. "*Qué pasa, amigo?*" he asked.

"Pardon, señor," the sergeant said. "It is the General's orders. You are to remain under guard. My name is Felix Nuñez."

So—Santa Anna liked him, but he didn't quite trust him.

"*Y mi amigo?* And my friend?"

"Under the care of Santa Anna's personal physician, Señor Reyes." Nuñez coughed dryly behind his hand. "Our medical corps, sadly, has proven nonexistent—contrary to what it says on the general's reports. Señor Reyes had to be hired at Saltillo when the general suffered an acute attack of stomachache—which cost us two weeks."

It wasn't just the medical corps, Tack soon discovered, that only looked good on paper; it was the entire army. Intrigue, discontent and graft were rife in this glittering Mexican army. The graft alone was downright appalling, what with Generals Gaona and Castrillón cornering all the supplies along the route and selling them back to the army at a mere 100 percent profit.

And Ramón Caro, Santa Anna's secretary, selling favors to the highest bidder; and Colonel Juan Almonte underselling Caro; and Colonel Ricardo Dromundo (another brother-in-law of Santa Anna's) knifing both of them in the back as he lined his own pocket.

And talk about discontent! Rotten pay and food, poor leadership, and no chance of a discharge unless killed. The Yucatán battalion, for instance: 70 percent Mayan Indians, savages who had been drafted into the army against their will and who couldn't understand word One of Spanish.

When the grand march for the Rio Grande was resumed, a private from Durango tried to desert. Tack expected Santa Anna to have the man shot or hanged when recaptured. No such thing. Santa Anna was far more cruel than that. He placed the man *back in the army*! The worst of all possible punishments: ten years in the army without pay!

The march started out with all the trappings and glitter of a Napoleonic conquest, the long rows of infantry in their white cotton pants and blue cloth jackets and tall black shakos (pompons and all), the proud dragoons with their slender pikes and glinting breastplates, the artillerymen in their pie-plate hats and white crossbelts, the haughty officers in navy-blue jackets with scarlet facings. . . .

It didn't stay that way for long. It fell apart at the seams.

On the upper benches of Monclova a wailing blizzard struck the grand army, wiping out the trail, blinding men and horses, losing the guides in the mesquite thickets. Troops and animals waded helplessly about in the snowdrifts, baffled by the sleet-driven winds that plastered them like snowmen.

Santa Anna—that military genius who thought of everything—had somehow forgotten to think about tents for the troops. Which meant that they had to huddle against one another in the snow-blasting nights for warmth. Which, to the Mayan troops from the hot tropics, didn't work out very well. They died by the scores.

"By Methuselah's nine hundred years!" Santa Anna cried at Tack (in the heated confines of his great tent). "Can't those stupid savages endure even a little frost?"

"But many of them don't even have blankets, General."

"Blankets! What are blankets to a soldier! Will it stop bullets? Can you eat it? Drink it? Paugh! I am killing myself to teach these troops that they are the greatest soldiers since Napoleon's legions! It is time they learned that—" Santa Anna paused and pointed at Tack.

"Put this down for your paper: The superiority of the Mexican soldier over the mountaineers of Kentucky and the hunters of Missouri is well known. Veterans seasoned by twenty years of war can't be intimidated by the presence of an army ignorant of the art of war, incapable of discipline, and renowned for insubordination! Do you have that? Now *that* is what I am trying to teach my men!"

The half-frozen, exhausted army dragged down the benches and into the mesas—to be confronted with more bad news. It had been a dry winter in the lowlands: very little water or grass for the livestock. The horses and mules and oxen quickly came down with *mal de lengua*, a swelling of the tongue caused by thirst and dry fodder. When they found water it was mostly stagnant and they died of a grim little disease called *telele*.

Nor were the troops faring any better. They fell by the wayside, victims of hunger and thirst. They tried to find nourishment in the adjoining fields, gulping down mesquite nuts and berries, and literally hundreds were stricken with dysentery. They dropped from sickness, from starvation, thirst, exhaustion. . . .

General Ampudia himself came to appeal to Santa Anna for the foundering troops.

"Give us a week, Excellence. Send out foraging details to find food for the troops."

Santa Anna snatched his foaming chapeau from his head and threw it into the parched sand.

"Jehoshaphat's second cousin! Stop when I've nearly reached my goal? Bog down here in this wilderness and give that filth-eater Houston a chance to build up his army? By the wooden leg of Moses, I'll march these troops till their tongues drag on the ground first! We're going on, General! *Comprender?*"

Yes, Ampudia understood all right, but the Comanches lurking in the sage and behind the rumples of land, didn't. They couldn't understand this invasion of what they considered as their land. So they sniped at the grand army, using arrows mostly, which you never heard coming. The soldiers continued to drop.

"If these soldiers keep falling out at this rate," Tack said to Tom, "there won't be a Mexican army by the time Santa Anna reaches Bexar."

"Don't fool yourself, boy. That Sergeant Nuñez told me thet Generals Sesma and Cós are waiting at the Rio Grande with their armies. They might not have much, but whatever they got will make up fer what Santy Anny's lost on this march."

"Cós! Why, he and his men are under parole to the Texans. He signed a capitulation not to fight us again."

Tom snorted and spat. "You think thet means shucks to Santy Anny? He makes up his own rules. And *he* says Cós will fight!"

Tack scratched at his neck. "Tom, we've been with this army long enough. It's time to get back to Bexar."

"Yeah? How? With no arms er hosses and Nuñez on us twenty-four hours a day like a watchdog over a bone?"

Tack thought for a moment, then said, "Listen. To-night . . ."

The mesa night was starbright as Tack and Tom walked toward the striped marquee. Their ever-present shadow, Nuñez, drifted after them. Tack turned around and said, "The general wants to see us."

Sergeant Nuñez nodded and hung back, but remained within sight. The two Texans approached the marquee sentry, and Tack said, "The general wishes to see us."

Tom stepped squarely before the sentry and delivered a short, penetrating knuckle jab to the man's solar plexus. The sentry went *Uuuh* quietly and started to fold at the middle. Tom propped him up, catching his musket before it could fall.

Tack removed the pistol from the sentry's belt, and looked back. It had been done quickly and quietly and in the dark no one, not even Nuñez, seemed aware of what the Texans were doing. Tom shoved the breath-paralyzed sentry through the tent flap. A moment later Tack followed them in.

The sentry had slumped to the ground, gasping for breath. Santa Anna, fussing with papers at his desk, looked up irritably.

"*Qué pasa?*" he snapped. Then he saw the pistol in Tack's hand and sprang to his feet. "Methuselah's idiot son! You must be mad!"

"Maybe," Tack said. "But we're getting out of here to-night."

"So! My suspicions were correct as usual. You are not a newspaperman but a spy!"

Tack shrugged. "Scout's a nicer word."

"Scout, spy, it's all the same to me—as long as you die in front of a firing squad." Santa Anna came around the desk and started walking toward Tack.

"You won't use that pistol. You're afraid to. The noise of it would bring half my army in here." He held out his hand, still advancing. "Give it to me."

Tack said nothing, did nothing. Santa Anna came up to him, sneering, his eyes beady and bold and cruel.

"You don't have the courage to use it. You are like all *Norte Americanos*. You lack the initiative of making instant decisions and acting upon them. That is why I shall crush you—all of you."

His hand darted out and snatched the pistol from Tack. He slapped the butt into his left palm and shoved the barrel against Tack's stomach and pulled the trigger. The lock went *clock*.

Santa Anna blinked, then rapped the muzzle against the sole of his boot to knock powder into the pan, cocked the lock and presented the barrel to Tack's stomach again and pulled the trigger.

Tack grinned. "You can stand there doing that all night. I drew the charge outside. You're right; we don't want any noise."

Santa Anna's face contorted with fury. He swung up the pistol, but Tom let the general have a swift jab in the back of the neck with the sentry's musket butt. Santa Anna collapsed like a bundle of guady clothing. "What now?" Tom wanted to know.

Tack started toward the rack of glittery uniforms.

"Pick out a uniform for yourself, Tom. These Mexicans don't know it yet, but two new generals are going to commandeer a couple of horses and get to heck out of here."

Tom spat at the general's silver chamber pot.

"Serves him right thet bump I give him on the back a his noggin. Yammer-yammerin' all the time about thet old fool Napoleon. Never once said a good word fer Gen'ril Arnold!"

10

DYING IS LIKE FALLING IN LOVE
FOR THE FIRST TIME

It was February 4 when Tack and Tom cantered down the Presidio Road and into the outskirts of Bexar. They were stopped by a squad of mounted Texans. Nap Mitchell was among them.

"Hoy, Tack! I thought you'd been skinned 'n' dried by the Mexicans by now. Stop aimin' pistols at 'em, you fellas! Tack 'n' me are the Mississippi army!"

"How are things here, Nap?" Tack asked. "Any changes?"

"Changes! That's all we've had is changes. Lemme tell you . . ."

Colonel Jim Bowie had arrived from Goliad on January 18 with thirty men. Houston had given him orders to go to the Alamo and demolish the fort. Houston's reason for this decision had been that the Alamo was too isolated to be held by a handful of Texans. But Bowie rarely acted upon another man's decision, general or not.

107

He and Colonel Neill put their heads together and asked each other this question: "Suppose we *don't* destroy the Alamo? What will the result be?"

The answer seemed obvious. Santa Anna would halt his advance into Texas to take the Alamo. He would have to do this because it was the way Napoleon would have done it. You never marched around an enemy position and left it in your rear to chop up your line of communication. So the Alamo would cost Santa Anna men and supplies and time.

And time was what Houston needed to create a Texas army.

Bowie decided to make a stand at the Alamo. He assumed command and put his handful of troops to work.

Almeron Dickinson, a Gonzales blacksmith, became the artillery captain. He had 19 fieldpieces and one 18-pounder to toy with. Green Jameson, the lawyer, became the Alamo's defense engineer. He constructed a log palisade across the chapel yard to fill in the gap between the church and the end of the compound's south wall. He built up earth-and-log platforms along the walls for gun mounts, and dug rifle pits and trenches outside the walls, and stockaded the main gate.

Bowie, meanwhile, was working like a man trying to move a mountain, sending couriers right and left to seek supplies and troops for the Alamo. He wrote provisional Governor Smith an urgent letter requesting help, stating:

> The salvation of Texas depends on keeping Bexar out of the hands of the enemy. It serves as the frontier picquet guard. . . . Colonel Neill and myself have come to the solemn resolution that we will rather die in these ditches than give it up to the enemy.

On February 3 Colonel William Travis arrived with thirty men. The governor had ordered him to Bexar to reinforce the Alamo, but Travis had marched under duress.

He didn't want to be stuck in an old mud fort in the middle of nowhere, nor did he appreciate being third man on the totem pole. Leadership, flair, action, were the qualities that motivated this dashing, melodramatic young lawyer.

So Travis came to Bexar with the sulks. But it was only a fleeting mood. The peculiar magic of the Alamo quickly captivated the intense young man, and before a week was out he was enthusiastically writing these lines to Governor Smith:

> It is more important to occupy this post than I imagined when I last saw you. It is the key to Texas. . . .

Tack rode into the stockaded outworks and through the tunnellike gate into the compound. He was surprised to see that the place was actually starting to look like a fort. Two 9-pounders faced him from a gun emplacement in the center of the Plaza. A logged ramp led up to a dirt platform in the southwest corner which housed the great 18-pounder. A flag belonging to the New Orleans Greys stood above the long barracks. A fieldpiece was being jockeyed into position in the chapel yard.

Volunteers had been dribbling into the Alamo for days, and the fort's force now numbered 142. Still, Tack thought, it was a mighty feeble amount to pit against Santa Anna's hordes.

A dandified officer strode up to Tack demanding his name.

"Tackett, sir. Scout for Colonel Neill."

"You can't see Colonel Neill," the captain said primly. "He's in Bexar. I'll take you to Colonel Travis."

Travis had black hair and black eyes. He was twenty-six and his face held the brooding intensity of a poet starving in a garret. He was dressed in homemade Texas jeans, pants and jacket.

"Yes, what is it, Captain Dimitt?" he snapped.

"One of Colonel Neill's scouts, sir—so he says. I've never seen him before."

"Colonel, I've been in Mexico for nearly a month," Tack said. "Santa Anna is on the march with 4,000 troops."

Travis brushed the news aside with an abrupt wave of his hand.

"Colonel Neill has been receiving reports that Santa Anna is within sight ever since you left here, Tackett. And Colonel Bowie has been receiving the same scare rumors ever since *he* arrived."

"Sir, this isn't a scare rumor. I was with the Mexican army."

"You were, eh?" Travis' tone implied disbelief. "Very well. Exactly where is the Mexican army at this moment?"

"I can't pinpoint it, sir. But Santa Anna was in Monclova on February first. By now he's—"

"By now he's probably not even as far as Saltillo," Travis imposed. "I know how a Mexican army moves. If you watch them for a whole minute you can actually see them take a step forward."

"Sir, if you believe that, then you don't know Santa Anna. He's a slave driver. He doesn't give a hoot about human life—except his own. He's deliberately marching half of his men to death in order to get the other half here to surprise you."

"Listen to me, Tackett." Travis' voice had an edge of exasperation. "I know Santa Anna is coming. We all know it. But not as soon as you expect. It will be mid-March at least before we see any sign of that gentleman."

"Pardon me, sir," Tack said doggedly, "but I think it's far more likely that we'll see him in mid-Feb—"

"That'll do, Tackett." His tone closed the interview. "Go find yourself some rations and a place to bunk."

Tack hesitated at the door.

"Sir? You'll give Colonel Neill my message?"

"Yes yes!" Travis turned back to his dispatches.

"What's wrong with that Travis?" Tack asked Hank. They were sitting on their bunks in the insect-infested shadows of the long barracks. Tack was eating rabbit stew: jack rabbit, he thought, from the way it was acting up in his stomach.

"He acts like he didn't believe that Tom Hendricks and I were with Santa Anna's army."

Hank shrugged. "I don't know. That's just his way. Intellectual and hardheaded. Has to do everything for himself. Won't take any man's counsel. And talk about stubborn! You heard how he started that trouble at Anáhuac in 'thirty-two? The Mexican commander took him prisoner, and when the Texans ganged up to come release him, the commander tied Travis to the ground and stood over him with a pistol; told the Texans he would kill Travis if they tried to release him.

"Can you imagine what that dramatic young man did then?" Hank asked. "He yelled at the Texans to go ahead and open fire. He would rather die on the spot than give in to the commander!"

The next day Tack met Jim Bowie.

Tack had been posted to guard duty on top of the hospital roof, the tallest building in the Alamo. He was standing under the wan winter sun, staring absently at Bexar, when he realized that someone was climbing the ladder from the roof of the low barracks.

A big-boned, craggy-faced man came over the edge of the parapet.

"Are you Tackett?" the giant asked. "I'm Bowie."

He had been a giant, in size and legend; but time, heartbreak, alcohol and sickness were undermining his structure. Now his face resembled a splendid head on a coin worn and

111

Bowie

dimmed until it was only a memory of sharpness and symmetry. But he was still Bowie—a living legend. Next to Boone, he was possibly America's greatest frontiersman.

The man and his knife both—the big hunting knife to which he had given his name; the man and the knife that had fought the famous Sand Bar Fight. Tack saw it hanging in its sheath on Bowie's hip.

But a grief-ridden man, who had become a Mexican citizen and married the nineteen-year-old María Ursula de Veramendi . . . only to have her and both their children die of the cholera in 1833. Then had come the long, tragic downhill tramp through an endless procession of whisky bottles; down to the bitter and lonely end where a moot sickness awaited him. A disease for which the doctors (such as they were) had no name. A disease that was slowly killing the giant.

"Is is true," Bowie asked Tack, "that Santa Anna [he pronounced it Santanna, in the Spanish style] reached Monclova on the first?"

"I was there with him, Colonel."

Bowie nodded, turning away. "Thanks," he said tonelessly.

"Sir," Tack called. "You believe me?"

Bowie looked back with a sort of half smile.

"Sure. Didn't Travis?" He grunted an explosive laugh. "I know Santa Anna too. If he was at Monclova on the first, then he'll be here by the 25th. Doesn't give us much time to—"

A great hullabaloo suddenly rang out from the compound below. Bowie and Tack stepped over to the parapet and looked down. Texans were running across the Plaza from everywhere, converging on the main gate. A smiling file of men were riding casually into the Alamo. Thirteen of them, led by a buckskin-clad man.

"Who is *that*?" Bowie growled.

Tack made a wry grin.

"That's our fourth colonel, sir. That's Davy Crockett and his Tennessee Mounted Volunteers."

Military discipline had gone by the boards. Tack deserted his post and joined the cheering Texans in the compound. After all, it wasn't every day that a man like Davy Crockett rode in to fight by your side. Some Louisiana boys presented Crockett with a soapbox and the colonel smilingly climbed up on it and started his speech.

"Boys, you see before you a homeless waif, a hungry

113

orphan. What I mean to say is, I been kicked out a Washington! Yessir! They run me out on a-count I had the gall, the unmitigated guts, to speak agin ol' Andy Jackson! So, boys, like hit er not, here I am! I'm knockin' kindly on your door and askin' fer room 'n' board!"

The Texans war whooped like fury.

We'll take you, Davy!

You kin have all our cactus juice 'n' rattlesnake meat you want!

How many Mexicans you figger you kin kill in one day, Davy!

Crockett, smiling benignly, held up his hand for attention.

"I jest want you to know, brothers, that I've come to your country not to gain votes ('cause what good are they to a politician who ain't runnin' fer any office?), but to aid you all I kin in your noble cause!

"Now! They call me 'Colonel' whar I came from (and a few other unsavory names besides), but you boys call me 'Davy' and that's how I want hit. As long as we're all here to defend the liberties of our common country, I don't wanta fight as a colonel. I jest wanta be a high private!"

More war whoops and cheers from the Texans. Crockett held up his hand again.

"Jest wanta mention to you boys what I told my Whig constituents when they kicked me out a Washington. I said to them: 'Brothers, as far as I'm concerned you kin go to—' "

Tack felt someone strike him on the arm. He turned and faced the irate-looking Captain Dimitt.

"Tackett, I posted you on guard. You're under arrest for deserting your post in time of war!"

Tack blanched. Conditions in the Texas army were so slipshod that he didn't yet quite understand military procedure.

"Why sir—" he fumbled, "I only came down like every-one else was doing, to see Colonel Crockett. There's not a guard at his post in this entire fort right at this moment."

"Yes," Captain Dimitt said snappishly, "and if I catch them I'll place *them* under arrest, too!"

Lou Rose shoved up to them, wearing a down-cornered smile.

"I wouldn't do that if I was you, Captain. Tack here's a friend of mine."

"And who do you think *you* are?" Dimitt asked pom-pously.

"Nobody much," Rose said, "just Colonel Bowie's best friend. Wait a minute, I'll call him over. Hey, Jim!"

"That's quite all right," Dimitt said hurriedly. "If the colonel excused Tackett from duty, it's quite all right." He turned and vanished into the crowd. Lou Rose grinned after him.

"Him and his pal Lieutenant Nobles is really a pair. A pair of deuces. They'll lick the boots of any man tagged with rank."

"Lou," Tack said, "are you really Colonel Bowie's friend?"

Rose gave him a sharp look. "What's wrong with you? You're starting to act like Hank—doubting everything I say. I *said* he was, didn't I?" He shoved off through the mob of Texans.

"Lou!" Tack called. "Wait a minute!" Then he realized that Nap was standing beside him, grinning about nothing.

"What's wrong, Tack?"

"I dunno. I never know how to take Lou. You've known him longer than the rest of us. How's he seem to you?"

"Lou?" Nap said. "Lou watches out for Lou. He's a pro-fessional soldier. That's the way they are."

"Is he really a friend of Bowie's?"

"Yep, believe it or not, he is. Bowie's strange. He'll take

115

to any fighter. Now Colonel Travis, he's like Hank. He hates the sight of Lou. Funny how we all think different, ain't it?"

Men kept dribbling in. . . .

Three brothers by the name of Taylor; David Cummings bringing rifles donated by his father; a young Tennessee boy called Asa Walker, who stole a coat and a rifle at Washington-on-the-Brazos in order to reach the Alamo clothed and armed, leaving a note of apology behind for his victim:

> . . . the hurry of the moment and my want of means to do better are all the excuse I have.

What nameless sense of urgency drove Walker on? He might just as well have quoted that old saying, *I run to death, and death meets me as fast.*

Others, already at the Alamo, also knew a sense of urgency. Nathaniel Kerr died of a fever. Lieutenant Ream was hurriedly trundled off to Gonzales because he had broken out with measles. Others deserted, by ones, by twos, as if the mere thought of the oncoming Mexican threat was too much for them. No one attempted to stop them. If they were that fainthearted, who wanted them?

David Cummings penned a letter to his father far-off in peaceful Pennsylvania:

> Many it is true have left the country and returned home to their friends and pleasures, but of such Texas has no use. . . . We want men of determined spirit that can undergo hardships and deprivation.

And the Alamo had them: 155 idealistic men, and still more star-crossed Americans were on their way. Hurrying, hurrying—to the showdown.

A fandango was held in Bexar on the 10th, to celebrate Crockett's arrival. The party was interrupted at midnight by a courier who rode in with a dispatch announcing (once again) that Santa Anna had been sighted. Colonels Bowie, Travis and Crockett went into a huddle and decided No, it was only another scare. Colonel Neill was not included in the huddle.

There was nothing wrong with Neill; but he didn't have Bowie's strength or Travis' drive or Crockett's flamboyancy. He seemed to sense that his star was in descension, and the following morning he turned the command of the Alamo over to Travis and took off for home on what he called "military leave."

"Well," Crockett said in his woodsy drawl, "thet helps some. Least now we won't all be stumblin' over colonels ever' time we turn around. I sware, four colonels fer 155 men is a powerful lot!"

But the troops failed to adopt his easygoing attitude. They saw no reason why they should serve under a twenty-six-year-old youth when they had the famous Jim Bowie among them.

"Is Neill out of his mind?" Rose raged. "Bowie's twice the man Travis will ever be! He should of left the command to Jim! He's let Jim do all the work and make all the decisions for the past five weeks, so why not give him full command?"

"Well, it doesn't really matter, does it?" Tack said. As far as he could see it was a case of Hobson's choice. None of the four colonels were real military men. Neill had been sedentary and undecisive; Bowie was brooding and sick; Travis was young and melodramatic; and Crockett seemed to be nothing but noise and lies.

Travis sensed the dissension, and—in his dramatic way —he cold-shouldered the military method and adopted the democratic manner: command by election.

"Who are you voting for?" Tack asked Hank.

"Travis," Hank said promptly. "He's the only one for the job."

117

"Aw for gadsake," Lou Rose growled. "Bowie is twice the fighter Travis is. Anybody knows that!"

"Maybe," Hank said. "But Bowie is a dying man. You can smell death on him."

Smell it or not, Bowie won the vote. But the election only concerned the volunteers; the regulars remained under Travis' command. It created a weird situation—two leaders: one commanding the majority, the volunteers; the other commanding the minority, the regulars. Like thieves, Bowie and Travis fell out. While the "high private," Crockett, kept his mouth closed and took command of the palisade in the chapel yard.

The following morning Bowie, sick, bitter, pie-eyed drunk, went raging into Bexar and made a complete fool of himself for hours. Tack and Nap and Lou Rose were ordered to go in and fetch him home. Lou immediately assumed command of the detail.

"Aw, Jim, Jim," he said when they found the shaggy giant lurching bewilderedly around in the Main Plaza. "Look at yourself, Jim. You've gone and insulted the citizens and let all the prisoners out of the calaboose and wrecked the town in general. What kind of way is that for a great man to act?"

Bowie, tall, gaunt, blear-eyed, stared at them with weary malevolence as he wavered like a lost ship in a rocking sea.

"A great man?" he echoed. "I might have been a great man. Might have been like Houston or Crockett. But I took the wrong turn somewhere, somewhere . . . I've seen too much, done too much. I've lost too much!"

He lurched forward and stumbled into Tack, his long hard arms finding support on Tack's shoulders. Groggily, he raised his head and looked into Tack's face.

"Who are—oh yes, you're the boy who's afraid, aren't you? Don—don't deny it. I saw it in your face that day on the hospital roof. You think I don't know the look when I see it? Afraid! Lish—listen, son, listen to me. You're going

118

to die. You know that, don't you? You're going to die with Jim Bowie. Bu—but don't be afraid. Dying is like falling in love for the first time. It's on you before you know it. You'll shee, you'll shee. I know . . . I know . . ."

Like falling in love, Tack thought, supporting the tragic, sick old giant. *But I've never been in love. . . .*

The next day Bowie went to Travis and made a deal: a joint command, all major decisions to be made together. They shook hands.

On that same day Santa Anna's soggy army crossed the Rio Grande under a torrential rain and joined up with General Sesma's force.

Santa Anna

II

THE RED FLAG MEANS
NO QUARTER

James Bonham was being sent to Goliad for help.

It was February 16 and Travis was growing nervous. Volunteers still dribbled into the Alamo, but the sick and the deserters still dribbled out. The number of the defenders remained about the same: roughly 150. Where in God's name were the reinforcements he expected?

Bonham would find them. Bonham would go to Fort Defiance in Goliad and get Colonel Fannin and his 420 troops. The defenders cheered as the South Carolinian started out on his 95-mile ride. Now they could breathe easier.

Colonel Fannin was the pride and joy of the new Texas army. He was an honest-to-gosh West Pointer! True—he hadn't actually graduated from the Point, but he'd had two years of extensive military training. He was busy drawing up a master plan for the defense of Texas when Bonham reached Goliad on the 18th.

"How are things at Bexar?" he greeted Bonham.

"Good. How soon are you marching?"

"Do what?"

"How soon can you reinforce the Alamo?"

Fannin pursed his lips. Well now, Mr. Bonham, he hadn't actually planned on coming to the Alamo. After all, he had no orders from General Houston or Governor Smith to that effect.

"Orders!" Bonham said. "Listen, Colonel, there's 150 of us in Bexar who haven't had orders to stay there and die. But we're going to stay, nevertheless."

Fannin was glad that Bonham had brought that up. He'd been thinking that perhaps it would be better to abandon the Alamo and have the defenders join him here at Fort Defiance. How did that idea strike Bonham? After all, this was a more compact fort than the sprawling Alamo, better situated, more organization . . .

"Remember to spell our names correctly," Bonham snarled as he stalked toward the door, "when you're an old retired general writing your war memoirs!"

The door slammed and Fannin rubbed at his face. The short, angry interview had left a sour taste in his mouth. If they could only understand the problems of command . . .

His restless eye fell on a copy of a dispatch he had written and sent to San Felipe ten days earlier. One line—his own words of assurance—leaped from the page at him:

> I will make such disposition of my forces as to sustain Bexar.

On the 16th, the 18th, the 20th, Travis received warnings from friendly Mexican riders that Santa Anna had crossed the Rio Grande. Travis ignored all three warnings. Sure, sure, he knew Santa Anna was coming, blast it all, *but not yet*. Santa Anna would wait for the spring grass: he would have to wait because of his cavalry. Travis still held to the belief that the Mexicans wouldn't arrive until the middle of March.

Tack was again on guard on the hospital roof. Captain Dimitt's pal Lieutenant Nobles had posted him there. They seemed to have it in for him somehow: always giving him the lousy details. He would much rather be out riding patrol with Nap and Hank than standing alone on this hot bare roof, or be down in the barracks grabbing some sack time like Lou Rose. Funny how Lou managed to miss all the fatigue details, how he could vanish like the snap of fingers whenever there was any work to be done.

The sun was up, whorling in a cloudless sky; under it lay Bexar, sprawling away. Gently swelling smooth fields in the lemon-yellow sun, like a slightly rumpled patchwork quilt on a giant bed, spread against the glittery apron of the San Antonio River. It was the day which last night had presaged—perfect spring, chill in the shadows, glassy clear. Powder House Hill and its hulking companions stood solid and separate, backed by the blank sky.

Tack's thoughts were in two levels. The upper level was this: *When we all go home from here, we'll be hailed as heroes. I'll be able to go back to my old job on the river. The old law won't dare pick on a national hero who fought in Texas. . . .*

The lower, the buried level, was this: *That little old outbuilding down there in the north corral might make a good hiding place. Nobody ever goes near it. You could dig a hole and cover it over with some boards and old hides, cache a little water and hardtack in there, and then when Santa Anna comes . . .*

He rubbed at his mouth, suddenly ashamed of his thoughts. Why couldn't he be more like his friends? Like Hank, dedicated and stoical; like Rose, tough and indifferent; or like Nap, just plain happy-go-lucky.

He looked down and saw Captain Dickinson's wife crossing the chapel yard with her little daughter Angelina. Mrs. Alsbury was with them. Mrs. Alsbury, though married to a "gringo" doctor, was Mexican.

122

There were many friendly Mexican families in the fort now, and their boisterous little offsprings simply overran the compound, the corrals and the barracks. Their mutt dogs, too.

Someone was riding a heavily burdened mule up the road to the fort. Tack yelled down at the guards inside the gate.

"Hey! Man coming up the road!"

The guards went out to meet the man on the mule, then fetched him into the compound. Tack could see that the newcomer was a Negro. One of the guards shouted across to the headquarters' sentry. "Tell Colonel Travis his servant's here from San Felipe!"

Tack started to turn away from the parapet, but stiffened and looked again. The Negro was plodding across the sunglazed plaza, leading his slope-eared mule to the corral.

It was Joe.

"What on earth are you doing here of all places?" Tack asked Joe. He was off duty now and they were standing in front of headquarters. Joe's grin was so white and wide it seemed to split his face in half.

"I never did git to Baton Rouge, Marse Tack. When I clumb outn dat ol' river I fell in wid some gemmums goin' to Texas to fight fo' liberty. So I come with 'em. Den I gits to San Fippy in Jan'ary an' de cunnel he finds me an' makes me his servant. Den he gits orders to come here, so he leaves me behind to collect all he gear an' fotch hit here to him."

"Well, Joe, I'm certainly glad to see you. Hank Warnell's here, too. He's out—" A rider came pounding through the gate and into the compound, drowning Tack's voice. It was old Tom Hendricks.

"Hey, Colonel! Come a-runnin'! Something's up in town!"

Travis and Bowie came to the door and Travis called for

123

his horse. Bowie looked dead on his feet. Whatever it was that was killing him was doing a good job of it.

"Get a horse, Tackett," Travis ordered. "I may need a courier."

Bexar was in an uproar. Mexican families were pouring out of the town and into the hills as if they thought the Day of Judgment had arrived. And in a way it had.

Helter-skelter, by wagon, horse, mule, foot—if that's all they could find—they rushed out of their houses clutching meager personal belongings, shouting at their bewildered children, herding off livestock, dropping pots and pans, running back for them. . . .

Travis and Tack and Tom started grabbing the stragglers.

"*Que pasa?* What's up! Where is everyone going?"

To visit relatives, señor . . . to do some farming, señor . . .

"Oh my aunt!" Tom growled. "Ain't nobody kin lie like a scared Mex. Visit relatives! Going farming! In February? Huh!"

Travis stopped a peasant who did not seem quite as panic-stricken as the others.

"In God's name what is happening here?"

"Santa Anna, señor. The townspeople have learned that his cavalry was only eight miles away last night."

A Dr. Sutherland joined them and the little group hurried up the bell tower of the San Fernando church. The empty mesquite-pegged plains rolled away from them in the warm stillness of morning sun. Tack couldn't see a thing. Neither could anyone else. Travis pursed his lips and shook his head.

"You two stay up here," he told Tack and Tom. He and the doctor went on down.

The morning sun inched onward. Noon came and the glare was deceptive. Then it was one o'clock. Tack, rubbing his aching eyes, heard Tom suck in his breath. "Got 'em!" the old-timer cried, and he sprang for the bell rope. Wide-eyed, Tack stared everywhere at once but saw absolutely nothing, no sign of life. The bell went *clong clong clong* over his head.

Travis and several others came ripping up the stairs. Tack still hadn't seen a blame thing and could only shrug when Travis cried "Where? Where?" And a few minutes later, some of them started jeering at old Tom.

"False alarm! Haw! Old One-Eye's seeing spots!"

"I seen 'em, I tell you!" Tom fumed. "They rid behint the brushwood!" But no one would believe him. The crowd dissipated.

"Tackett," Travis said, "you ride out the Larado Road with Doc and check on Hendricks' eyes—I mean eye."

Tack and Doc Sutherland cantered down the road about a mile and a half out of town and urged their mounts up to the spine of a razor-backed hill. The Mexicans were there all right—370 of Sesma's dragoons in their sun-sparked breastplates, waiting impatiently in the brushwood for orders.

"*YAH!*" Tack and Doc were off in a cloud of red dust and flying shale, slamming down the slope. They hit the bottom together and Doc's bay lost its footing and crashed to its knees, Doc spinning ankles over appetite into a smokebush.

Lordy! Tack wheeled about and trotted back, leaped from his pony, helped punchy Doc to his feet and got him mounted. Then they were off again, charging way-hey for town.

Old Tom saw them flying up the road and he started clonging the bell again. No one doubted this warning. The town burst into frantic activity, like a beehive that's just received a swift kick. Foot soldiers, horsemen, wagons, went banging down the streets and across the old footbridge, everyone running for the Alamo.

An old Mexican woman looking out her window at the tide of Texans sweeping by, called, *"Pobre hombres.* Poor men, you will all be killed."

The defenders came piling back into the Alamo and to Tack it was like rushing into a madhouse: kids crying, hysterical Mexican mothers snatching them up, dragging them along by the hand; officers bawling themselves hoarse with unheeded orders, volunteers running here, there, everywhere; a herd of cattle stampeding into the north corral, filling the air with resounding *mooo-uhs*; Dickinson and his artillerymen carting up shot and powder for the great 18-pounder.

Bowie and Rose led a squad into the depressed area called La Villita—a ratty collection of huts not far from the Alamo—and grabbed up whatever they could find that might prove useful—mostly sacks of grain. The women and children and other noncombatants were herded into the empty rooms of the old Alamo church.

No one bothered to give Tack any orders, so he turned his nag into the south corral, took his shotgun and climbed up to his usual post, the hospital roof. A most unpleasant sensation was active in his stomach. It felt like a fleet of little icebergs bumping about in there. This was what the Spaniards called *la Hora de la Verdad*. The Hour of Truth —the supreme moment when a man's real nature is expressed and exposed in a single gesture. He runs, or he stands.

Hank Warnell was trotting across the roof of the long barracks. He looked mighty grim around the mouth.

"Hey, Hank!" Tack called. "Up here!"

Hank stopped and looked up, his face a mask of outrage.

"Do you know what those two bully boys Captain Dimitt and Lieutenant Nobles just did?" he shouted. "Deserted! I saw them go over the wall. Filthy cowards!"

Big loss, Tack thought. He for one wouldn't miss them. They had faced their Hour of Truth.

Travis scribbled another hurried appeal to Fannin for help and handed it to a young fellow from Wales—Lewis Johnson. "Ride like the wind, boy," he said.

Just then Davy Crockett came into the office half-supporting Doc Sutherland. Doc had wrenched his knee when his horse spilled him. He could barely walk.

"Colonel," Crockett said, "here I been in this war-torn Texas territory fer three weeks, and now I'm finally goan see me a Mexican soldier. What you want me and my boys to do?"

"Think the thirteen of you can hold the chapel yard palisade?"

"Hold it? Shucks, Colonel, you talkin' about Tennessee boys. We kin pick hit up and march hit down to Mexico."

Travis grabbed a quill and a sheet of paper.

"Doc, you won't be any use to us here with that knee. But you can ride, eh? Get this dispatch to Gonzales." Rapidly, he wrote:

> The enemy in large force is in sight. We want men and provisions. . . . We have 150 men and are determined to defend the Alamo to the last. Give us assistance.

He addressed it TO ANY OF THE INHABITANTS OF TEXAS.

General Santa Anna was in a lousy temper. The night before, he had ordered Sesma and his dragoons to hit Bexar with a surprise attack. And what had that idiot Sesma done? He had halted only a mile or so from town and sat there all night! And why had the idiot done this? *Nombre de Dios,* because he was afraid the stupid Texans were going to attack *him*! Such a *nuez* (nut)!

Now it was 3 P.M. and Santa Anna was herding his dragoons and infantry into Bexar's Military Plaza. He turned into the Main Plaza and dismounted amid the cheers of his troops. Heading for his headquarters, the Yturri

House, his band blared trumpet and tuba noises at him while the proud flags flapped over his head.

Flags? By Jonah's seasick stomach, His Excellency would show those Texas rebels what it meant to fool with General Santa Anna!

"*El rojo! El rojo!*" he snapped at a coronet.

Tack, 800 yards away on top of the hospital roof, saw a great red flag unfurl from the San Fernando bell tower. It was caught by an afternoon breeze and whipped at its staff. A hush fell on the Alamo.

"What's that mean?" Tack called over to Lou Rose. Lou grunted, staring balefully at the distant flag.

"The red flag means No Quarter."

"No Quarter? You mean No Surrender?"

"That's it. Even if we wanted to surrender, they wouldn't let us. That old he goat Santa Anna means to kill us to the last man."

Abruptly the Alamo made its reply to the red flag. The 18-pounder kicked with a roar, lobbing a cannon ball into Bexar.

Doc Sutherland, now in the hills, heard the shot and decided it was time to make hasty tracks to Gonzales. James Bonham, in the same hills, heard it and knew it was time to get back into the Alamo. He met Lew Johnson in a limestone gulch. They shouted at each other in passing.

"What's up?"

"Everything! Mexicans have showed! I'm off to Fannin for help!"

"Waste of time!" I've tried!"

"Orders! Luck, Mr. Bonham!"

Luck to all of us, Bonham thought, as he came pounding down the draw and into the fields and aimed for the distant fort.

It was the afternoon of February 23.

128

I2

WHAT TRAVIS AND BOWIE
ARE TRYING TO DO ISN'T
TACTICALLY SOUND

Tack reported to Colonel Bowie's quarters as ordered. Bowie was sitting on his cot and he looked like death warmed over. He handed Tack a piece of paper—a page from a child's copybook.

"You know Santa Anna. Get yourself a white flag and take this to him."

The icebergs in Tack's stomach collided violently. Bowie studied him for a moment, then said, "Read it."

Tack skimmed through the penned lines. The message was a question: Were the Mexicans seeking a truce? Tack didn't understand. Bowie made a down-cornered smile.

"It's only a stall for time. They don't want a truce any more than we do. You're not afraid to take it, are you?"

Tack shook his head and managed to lie. "No sir." Not much!

He went into town with a white napkin tied to a stick. A Colonel Batres took the message from him and delivered it to Santa Anna. Tack was just as glad. He had no desire to come face to face with His Excellency again—flag of truce or not.

Santa Anna couldn't believe the sheer effrontery of the message. *He* should come to terms, when his magnificent army overpowered the stupid Texans forty to one? He dictated a terse reply: Unconditional surrender was the only option he would offer.

Tack started back to the Alamo with the reply—only to meet a young captain from Tennessee, Albert Martin, coming out. They stopped on the footbridge and compared notes.

Travis, infuriated that Bowie would try to open negotiations with the Mexicans without first consulting him, was sending his own courier. Tack showed Martin his reply from Santa Anna.

"Not much sense in prolonging this, then," Martin said.

"No, sir. When Santa Anna says Unconditional Surrender, that's just what he means."

That night, the first night of the siege, started out badly —significantly, too—for the defenders of the Alamo. Travis had had his feelings hurt and he didn't mind implying as much to Bowie. They argued. Crockett tried to pacify. The other officers looked on apprehensively. Obviously when the chips were down, a joint command between this sensitive colonel, Travis, and this stubborn colonel, Bowie, would not work.

And right at that crucial moment fate stepped quietly in and laid a heavy hand on Bowie. He collapsed. The fort's surgeon (actually he was only a medical student) didn't know what to make of Bowie's malady. First he diagnosed consumption, then changed his medical opinion to typhoid; one way or another, Bowie had had it. He turned over the command to Travis and was put to bed.

The morning of the 24th started out with a slam—cannon slam.

The Mexicans were busy digging earthworks about 400

yards away, along the riverbank. They opened the siege with three guns: a 5-inch howitzer and two 9-pounders. The shells screamed gaudily into the Alamo. Dickinson and Bonham replied with the three 12-pounders mounted on the ramp inside the church.

Hank joined Tack on the hospital roof. They ducked in unison each time a Mexican shell whanged overhead. There was a 9-pounder up there with them but no one bothered to fire it. The Texans were conserving their powder.

A shell crashed into the north corral and a badly wounded brown-and-white cow went bawling around the enclosure. Tack and Hank both started to lift their guns, when Lou Rose entered the corral and shot the suffering beast dead with his Elgin pistol.

"You wouldn't think Lou had that much sympathy for animals," Hank said as he lowered his rifle.

"I dunno," Tack said. "He's a funny man. You never know how he feels. Maybe he likes animals better than people. Soldiers and frontiersmen are often that way."

The shells continued to fall into the fort all through the day. But it was a great waste of shot and powder. Net result for a few hundred rounds of cannon shot: one dead cow. The Mexican artillerymen, however (searching for laurels), claimed they had killed four of the Alamo defenders; and Santa Anna, always eager to believe anything that furthered his cause, praised them highly.

The Mexicans ceased fire at sunset, and Travis put this lull to good use. First he sent Launcelot Smithers off with a report on the estimated strength of the enemy, then he penned the most famous dispatch to come out of the Alamo.

> Fellow citizens and compatriots: I am besieged by 1000 or more Mexicans. . . . I have sustained a continual Bombardment for 24 hours and have not lost a man. The enemy demands a surrender at discretion,

otherwise, the garrison is to be put to the sword. . . . I have answered with a cannon shot, and our flag still waves proudly from the walls. I shall never surrender or retreat. I call on you in the name of Liberty, patriotism and everything dear to the American character, to come to our aid. . . .

Melodramatic? Maybe. Yet the words "everything dear to the American character" seem to justify Travis' theatrical plea. He was calling to the people who had put the word Liberty on the map.

He addressed his message TO THE PEOPLE OF TEXAS AND ALL AMERICANS IN THE WORLD. Then he handed the dispatch to Albert Martin, and the young captain whanged out of the fort like a shot.

To Sesma's dragoons Martin was just another of the Alamo's many pesky messengers. They shrugged in their Latin manner and let him go. Santa Anna had more important matters up his sleeve. . . .

In the evening the Mexican band came down to the river and began to make pretty music for the Texans. In place of kettle drums, Santa Anna (always thoughtful) would have his soldiers lob an occasional grenade at the fort. It was all very lulling.

Tack, listening dreamily to the music, thought of the Mississippi and wondered what old Ben Burrows was up to. Suddenly he stiffened, staring at the river. Something was moving down there in the dark.

"Mexicans attacking across the footbridge!" he yelled.

It was the Tennessee Mounted Volunteers' meat. Crockett and his boys opened with their deadly long rifles. They chopped up the little night party, knocking the officer, Colonel Bringas, off the bridge and chasing him through the black water with their bullets.

"By grabbit!" Crockett yelled. "Ifn I'd knowed there was

this kind a excitement here, I'd a come to Texas afore I went to Washington!"

The morning came in with a drizzly dawn and showed the Alamo defenders that the Mexicans had not been idle during the night. More and more earthworks had been thrown up, and howitzers had been jockeyed into position. The Mexican bugles filled the air with shrill wailing notes, and their artillery let loose with grape and langrage—bolts and nails and musket balls and bits of chain—which came *zzzm zzzm-ing* at the fort.

The Mexican infantry started to advance, darting in and out of the adobe huts and board-walled shanties of La Villita. The Texans loaded their cannons with canister (small projectiles in a case), and watched the Mexicans come—shack by shack, closer and closer. Crockett signaled with his open hand: Hold your fire.

Less than 300 feet away . . . Crockett made a fist of his hand, jerked it above his head and swept it down. The Alamo's cannons kicked back with a belch of smoke and shot. The Texans cheered and rushed to the palisade to join Crockett's riflemen.

The Alamo's canister tore into the shanties, into the advancing Mexican troops. The Tennessee sharpshooters called their shots:

See the filler with his third button missin' on his jacket? Pow! A brand-new round buttonhole.

The Mexicans flew head over heels, came apart, slammed into walls. Canister does that to troops. They went down in bunches, screaming and kicking and carrying on something awful. Sometimes a clenched hand would rise out of a fallen clump of soldiers, as if cursing all men. One man, crawling on his knees and tearing at his jacket front, reminded Tack of the gut-busted cow he'd seen the day before. Some of the Mexicans stumbled around through the clots of dead and dying like men bewildered in a fog, seemingly lost in the burning reek of powder smoke.

They retreated—what was left of them; the Texans bapping away at the fleeing figures with their rifles and muskets. A great cheer came from the Alamo. Crockett waved his coonskin cap on the end of his rifle. Lou Rose grunted and reloaded his shotgun.

"Listen to the dummies," he commented to Tack. "They ain't got the sense to realize that our turn is coming soon."

Tack, powder-streaked and excited, looked at him.

"What do you mean, Lou?"

"Mean what I've learned as a soldier. Ain't no side ever had any battle all its own way. Our turn is coming to be hit—hit hard."

That night Tack, Robert Brown, Charles Despallier, James Rose, Nap Mitchell, Hank Warnell and Tom Hendricks reported at headquarters. Travis told them the situation, gave them their orders.

"La Villita must be destroyed. The Mexicans can plant batteries in those shacks and blow the Alamo to shreds. I want that area leveled to ash."

Trouble was, Tom Hendricks was certain that there were still plenty of Mexican snipers lurking in the shanties. He suggested that the artillerymen give them cover fire. Dickinson's men sprayed La Villita with grape. Then the gate swung open and Tack and the others went racing into the night with firebrands.

A musket went *pow* somewhere in the dark ahead. Tack ducked and swerved to the left, and the next thing he knew he had reached the nearest buildings in one piece. The rat-haunted black shanties hulked around him like somber night monsters. The smoldering flame of his torch showed him empty windows, gaping doors, sagging roofs. He sprang to an adobe wall and thrust his torch under the overhang of thatch. It caught with a crackle and blazed up like cornstalk in July. He ran to the next hut.

Nap went by him, his grinning mouth agleam in the dancing light, and vanished down a lane. Robert Brown was yelling something, somewhere. Tack painted a dry wooden wall with flame, got it going good, and trotted around a corner . . . nearly into the grabbing hands of a Mexican captain who leaped from the shadows like a jack-in-the-box.

Tack sidestepped hurriedly and swung his torch at the Mexican's contorted face. In the weird light the man's eyes looked mad. He fell back, cursing.

Tack saw a sword slither from its scabbard. The blade shone, the thin red light from the torch dancing along the edge like blood. For a moment they tried to fence like that —the firebrand against the sword. Then Tack cocked the torch over his shoulder and tossed it like a racing comet at the Mexican's head.

He ducked out of there, hearing Hank yell, "Enough! Enough! Fall back to the fort!"

It was like running out of an inferno: each rutty little lane a splash of yellow flame, each tawdry little shack a crimson bush of fire, and the night was filled with showering sparks like blazing snowflakes. The incendiaries raced into the sheltering dark, leaving La Villita behind like a fiery dragon, writhing and coiling, hissing out great belches of lurid smoke.

General Santa Anna, standing high in the San Fernando tower, put his fingers to his face and clawed at his flesh. Just look at what his idiot infantry had allowed to happen! La Villita burning, and now a norther—one of those mean icy Texas winds—was wailing across the prairies to help fan the flames!

The general came down from the tower to the Main Plaza, where his glittery array of officers waited apprehensively, and pulled his plume-foamy hat from his head and threw it into the mud and gave it a good kick and, for a moment, almost gave in to the impulse to snatch out a pistol and take a shot at it. Or someone.

"Jezebel's whalebone girdle! Must I take care of everything myself? Can I trust no man to do a simple little task? By Elijah's fiery overcoat, now we've lost the best possible position for mounting a battery! I want at least five new batteries dug in by tomorrow night at this time! I want the Alamo hemmed in with batteries! I want—"

"*El Presidente!*" A breathless courier rushed across the plaza. "The Alamo has just sent out two more messengers!"

Santa Anna sighed. He stared at the ground. He hummed a few bars of *La Cucaracha*. Why was he cursed with such a worthless army? How was it possible that his witless soldiers (whom he had trained himself) could allow the Texan couriers to go trotting in and out of the Alamo any time they felt like it?

"This must cease! No more enemy messengers to go in or out of that accursed Alamo! Train batteries on them, if you must! Bring them down with grape! I want this nonsense stopped!"

It was lucky that Tack and Captain Juan Seguin got away when they did; for they were the two messengers. Travis hadn't said anything to anyone but secretly he was beginning to realize the hopelessness of his situation. Too many Mexicans, too many heavy guns. He *had* to have reinforcements! He wrote to Sam Houston:

> Hasten aid to me as rapidly as possible . . . from the superior number of the enemy, it will be impossible for us to keep them out much longer

Now—who was to carry it? None of the officers seemed in a great hurry to volunteer. They put their heads together and railroaded Captain Seguin into the job. He accepted stoically.

136

"Take young Tackett with you," Travis said. "He's a good rider. If you both reach the hills, send him on to Fannin in Goliad."

Seguin collected Tack and borrowed Bowie's horse. Bowie himself was so wild with fever he didn't seem to recognize Seguin. . . . Sure, take it, take any blame thing. He didn't care.

A rain-ribbed wind was sweeping the night. The gate flew open and Tack and the captain went driving out, a sentry on the wall yelling after them, "Lucky!"

My foot, Tack thought. They went jinglety-jink, jinglety-jink across the porous fields, forded the chuckling creek and turned toward the Gonzales road. "Slow now, amigo," Seguin warned. Tack reined his bay down to a brisk walk. He knew they were approaching a Mexican outpost. A group of dismounted dragoons were lazying about the side of the road with a bit of a fire for warmth. They heard the two horsemen coming and called a challenge: *Quién es?*

"*Hermanos!*" Seguin replied. Brothers in arms. "Ride like the very devil when we reach the light," he whispered to Tack. The glare of the fire crept toward them like a little island of spreading light. The dragoons' breastplates gleamed. Seguin hunched over.

"*Ahora!*" Now! They booted home and bolted by the startled sentries, the black wall of night beyond the fire charging toward them like the ultimate edge of the world.

Pak pak pak! Carbines and curses crackled after them. *Arriba!* Mount up! After them! Tack and Seguin went pounding down the old road, Seguin calling, "Turn off! Get to Fannin! *Vaya con Dios!*"

Tack swung his bay's head and fled into the southeast, with two or three dragoons boiling along far back in his wake. He rode toward an unseen dawn. It was the last he ever saw of Juan Seguin.

On padded feet the night prowlers crept from their hiding holes and slunk away at the sound of Tack's throbbing approach. Owls and bats whipped by on silent wings, the owls straight and true, the bats erratic in flight. Weird and wild the yucca and cacti plants reared out of the cold darkness and were instantly swept aside. Little voices chittered in the night—strange murmuring phantom voices, as though the old, old badlands were haunted by the dim ghosts of savages and priests, conquistadors, prospectors and pioneers, now all gone, long gone. The glazed herd of stars above the peaks and ridges were lonely and far away.

Tack rode on.

The gray of the new dawn changed to yellow to pink to flaming rose. The vague mesquite thickets assumed definite shapes and the detail of the lumpy rocks emerged in the light like shaggy bears. Tack went up on a hogback and looked back along his trail. The prairie stretched away to the limits of its horizon. Void of life. He had shaken the dragoons sometime in the night.

He rode into the morning. The only active sign of life he saw that day was two wild turkey gobblers dancing around and around in combat to the tune of some unheard strain.

Late that night he encountered manmade activity—the little bright pinpoints of many campfires in the moony distance. Colonel Fannin was on the march.

Fannin, with 320 men and four cannon, had left Goliad that morning to come to the Alamo's relief. But things had gone wrong. . . .

Right off the bat three wagons had broken down. The army had stopped to make repairs. Then they found that a single team of oxen wasn't enough to haul the heavy guns across the river. More time lost in rigging double hitches. It rained, the wind howled. Night caught Fannin with a divided force: his cannon on one side of the river, his ammo wagons on the other. He ordered a bivouac.

He didn't have enough trouble? His pickets dozed and all the oxen meandered off into the night to look up some tasty

138

bunch grass. Tack rode into camp and found himself in the center of a very dispirited little army. The officers were holding a council of war.

"I'm Tackett from the Alamo," he offered the council. "I'm surely almighty relieved to find you gentlemen on the march."

No one said anything for a moment. They seemed to be avoiding his eyes.

"Sit down," Colonel Fannin said heavily. "We've just been discussing the advisability of continuing the march."

Tack thought he had heard wrong. "The advisability?"

Fannin nodded. "Our supply situation is bad. Only half a barrel of rice and no beef to speak of, except for our wagon and gun teams."

Tack looked at the gloomy, mute officers. They kept their eyes averted.

"Colonel," he said, "I know it's no fun marching on an empty stomach, but Santa Anna's men came all the way from Saltillo on half-rations of hardtack and mesquite nuts."

"Yes," Fannin said, "but there's more than just chow to be considered. We're only 320 men with four cannon and not much ammo. What can we possibly do against three or four thousand Mexicans?"

"*Do!* You—you can—" Tack tasted a wild wave of anger in his throat. He paused and swallowed, forced it down. "But, sir, *we're* only 150 men in the Alamo! We had two months before Santa Anna showed up in which to run, but we didn't. Four days ago we could have surrendered on his terms if we'd wanted to, but we didn't."

Fannin frowned. "I appreciate that, son, but you have to appreciate the fact that what Travis and Bowie are trying to do isn't tactically sound. I was taught at West Point that a—"

Tack couldn't hold it any longer.

"Tactically sound! Hopping Hannah! We're making a

139

stand at the Alamo in order to slow down Santa Anna, so that General Houston will have time to organize an army. We've already cost the Mexicans four days! Don't you consider *that* tactically sound?"

"I consider it splendid," Fannin said gently, as though dealing with an idiot child who could not grasp a simple arithmetic problem. "But you must see the over-all military picture. If we go to Bexar we will leave Goliad undefended. And Goliad is the stronghold of Texas."

"But the Alamo is the cornerstone of the rebellion," Tack argued. "Santa Anna himself admitted that."

"Well, yes—but—" Fannin seemed to waver.

Just then a commotion started in the dark. A rider was coming in. He was mud-daubed and trail-whipped but you could hear him yelling his news all over camp.

"General Urrea's Mexicans caught Colonel Johnson's Matamoros expedition at San Patricio! Only fifty miles south a here! Johnson got away but all the rest a the expedition was massacred. I tell you, boys, them Mexes ain't takin' *no* prisoners!"

It was enough for Fannin's tactical West Point mind. He jumped to his feet bawling orders.

"Pack up! Fall in! We're retreating to Fort Defiance. This news justifies our retrograde movement. We must defend Goliad at any cost!"

Tack stood there with the bugles blaring in his ears, with the soldiers rushing everywhere around him striking camp and grabbing up blankets and pans and rifles. Retrograde, he thought. An almighty fancy word for running away. Then he let out his breath and walked over to his fagged horse.

A captain wearing a sheepishly concerned expression stopped him.

"Don't you want something to eat before you ride out?"

"No," Tack told him. He mounted up and started the long ride back to the Alamo.

13

IF I CAN DIE IN HERE,
WHY CAN'T YOU?

It was the morning of the 28th. Tack had stopped to water himself and his nag at a little creek which gurgled over a white limestone bottom. He heard the clop-clack of hoofs on stones and snatched his shotgun from the saddle scabbard, but relaxed when he spotted the rider coming up the draw. It was nineteen-year-old Ben Highsmith, one of the Alamo's defenders.

"Anything wrong, Ben?"

Ben dismounted with a bone-aching grunt and started rubbing his saddle-sore seater.

"Depends on what you call wrong. Travis was feared you 'n' Seguin wouldn't git through, so he sent me out fer help. The Mexes is still creepin' closer with their stinkin' batteries and blowin' billy-be-durned outn the Alamo. Bonham led a sortie agin some a Gen'ril Sesma's men. A whole batch a Mex families what was in the Alamo has slipped away and jined Santy Anny. And Richard Allen led another raid agin La Villita."

141

"Allen?" Tack said. How that boy had changed since the Bucket a Bombs incident!

"Well, Fannin isn't going to relieve us, so there's no sense in you going on. Let's get back to the fort." Tack mounted up and looked down at Ben.

Ben hadn't made a move. He averted his eyes when he spoke.

"I been thinkin', Tack. If we go back we'll git ourselves kilt, likely. Ain't much sense in thet, is they? We're out a hit now. Why not stay thetaway?"

Yeah, Tack suddenly thought. *Why not? Why go back and stick my head in Santa Anna's noose? If I don't go back, I'll probably live through this blame war. And I've already done my share, haven't I? If I do go back, I'll die in the Alamo. . . .*

Rationalization loves company. Ben saw that Tack was weakening and he hastily tried to win him over to his way of thinking.

"They're just goan die in thet rabbit-hutch fort, Tack."

He was like a man who realizes he has holes in his self-esteem; he was rushing up wheelbarrow after wheelbarrow of excuses to fill in the pits.

"You 'n' me both know hit. Ain't nuthin' kin save 'em. They're as good as daid right now. Ain't they, Tack? Ain't they?"

They, Tack thought. Travis, Bowie, Crockett, Hank, Nap, old Tom, all of them. They—his friends—were going to die in the Alamo. *Lord,* he said, *tell me what to do.*

Then he realized that he had no decision to make. It had been decided for him a long time ago: the day he met Hank. It wasn't a question of smart or stupid or right and wrong; it wasn't actually even a matter of patriotism or cowardliness. You had to do the thing you believed in. And Tack believed in his friends. It was as simple as that. He felt greatly relieved.

"See you, Ben," he said. He nudged the bay and started down the draw, Ben's voice following him.

"You slab-sided fool! You'll never even git in! Santy Anny's got the fort ringed in solid!"

Tack left the mesquite thickets and started up a rocky incline, all stained with splashes of gray and orange and red and yellow lichens, and on up to the ridge. From the top of Powder House Hill he looked down on the distant Alamo. Dusk was swiftly claiming the prairie and a coyote saluted the encroaching night with his high lonesome *Howwww*. The dazzle of campfires showed that Santa Anna's troops were much closer now to the Alamo.

Occasionally a sharpshooter's rifle would cough. That was all. Tack turned down into an arroyo—and into an ambush.

"Hold it, amigo, or you're dead," a cold voice said.

Tack looked around and saw three-four men step out of the scrub with leveled rifles. They were all Texans. They looked it, too.

"My name's Tackett. One of Travis' couriers. Who're you?"

They were George Kimball's volunteers, 32 of them from Gonzales. Captain Albert Martin was with them. So was David Cummings who had been caught out of the fort when the siege began and had been looking for a safe way back in ever since.

"He's all right," Martin told them. "I know him. He's done more than ten men to hold Bexar since the first of December."

Funny the happy glow Martin's words gave Tack; gave him a sense of belonging. For the first time he felt that he was coming home—home to the Alamo.

"Let's go," Kimball said. "Mount up."

To look at him in the dusk you would think he was a big

rough-and-tumble western brawler. But he wasn't. He was only a simple hatter from New York. He had a wife and child in Gonzales.

The 33-man troop came out of the hills in the norther-blowing dark and cantered across the black fields, striking for a blank spot between the smoky fires of Sesma's corps. Suddenly a mounted silhouette appeared in their path—a slim man sitting tall in the saddle, as sharply defined as if he were clipped out of black tin.

"Do you wish to enter the Alamo, gentlemen?" he asked quietly.

The Gonzales volunteers hesitated. Captain Martin answered.

"Yes. Can you lead us?"

"Follow me," the mystery man said. He wheeled about and trotted on ahead of them. Tack pulled up alongside John Smith, an old frontier scout.

"What do you think?"

"Lots a things, boy," Smith muttered. "He speaks the wrong kind a English for these parts, for one thing. Ain't nobody goan call us 'gentlemen.' Not even Travis. Another thing: he don't tell us who he is. And mind the fat distance he keeps 'tween him 'n' us. George!" Smith whispered at the black figure of Kimball. "I don't trust thet new guide a ourn, George. Like as not he'll lead us right into a Mex encampment."

"What do you suggest we do?" Kimball whispered.

"Put him to a lee-tle test," Smith said. Suddenly he roared in a great voice. "Boys, hit's time to put some bullet holes in thet fella!"

Their self-appointed guide booted in his spurs on instant reflex and shot off into the black mesquite thickets, shouting, *"Fuego, amigos!"* Fire!

"Ride, boys, ride!" Smith yelled.

Tack spurred his bay and went off in a glory of tossed mud, Kimball's troop banging right after him. Off to the left a volley of shot crackled in the night. Then, reaching, throwing, going, the hoofs of the bay chopping at the inky turf underfoot, Tack saw the stark walls of the Alamo rising in the dark.

"Yo!" he yelled. "Americans coming in!"

But the Alamo defenders were wary of Santa Anna-type tricks by now and a Kentucky rifle went *pamm* from the wall and one of the bucketing Gonzales riders caught the slug in the foot. His instantaneous reaction to this warm welcome was so typically Texan that no one could doubt his nationality.

"Hairless Hatty's hatbox! Knock hit off! If I catch the turnip-head that fired that shot I'll turn him toes over nose!"

"Hi!" Crockett's voice rang out. "Cease fire! Don't you mudhaids know a American when you hear one swearin'?"

The main gate swung open and Tack led the mounted rush into the compound. Travis was at his stirrups before he could dismount.

"For mud's sake, Tackett. This can't be *all* of Fannin's force!"

"No sir. This is Kimball's volunteers. Fannin isn't coming."

Travis turned away shaking his head. "What is wrong with those fools? What do they expect of us? If Santa Anna overpowers us, we will fall here as a sacrifice at the shrine of our country. Is that what they want from us—immolation?"

The words stayed in Tack's ears: *immolation*—to sacrifice one's self. *The shrine of our country.* . . .

He looked around at the dark old walls of the Alamo. Was it possible? Would this place one day become a shrine, because of what he and Travis and Bowie and Crockett and all the others were doing?

Again he sensed the nameless, mute enchantment of the Alamo. And now he knew that many others had sensed it

145

as well. Bowie had come to blow it up; Travis had come under orders, against his own will; Crockett had come to do some hunting; Bonham had come because Mobile had sent him; and Tack had come only because of his friends.

Yet they had all stayed when they didn't have to. Why? What was the magical draw of this place?

Then Lou Rose came up and caught the bay's reins and broke Tack's contemplation.

"You fool. Ain't you learned nothing from me? Why didn't you stay out of this trap when you had the chance? You must be hankering for a Mex bayonet."

The dawn illuminated the damp stage of a regular siege.

It was the 1st of March. It had been raining. Bonham had been sent out to carry another call for help. Santa Anna's artillery had crept within 250 yards of the fort and the conflict had settled down to a grim business of snipers and shells.

The Mexican artillery never let up. It pound-pound-pounded at the Alamo's aged walls. The Alamo's sharpshooters never let up either. The fort not only had Crockett's deadly Tennessee long riflemen, it also had its fair share of Kentucky and Virginia and Pennsylvania marksmen.

They were wicked, all of them. They squatted behind the parapets on the walls, with four-five loaded rifles handy per man, and every time they saw a flicker of movement in the Mexican lines they whapped a bullet into it.

A sentry called Crockett's attention to a Mexican engineer who was considering the possibility of a new gun emplacement on the east side of the river. Crockett glanced over the wall, then strolled on down to the Alamo's southwest corner, went up the ramp and hunkered beside the 18-pounder. He took a sight and fired.

It was a 200-yard shot and the engineer dropped dead. Crockett stood up and calmly reloaded his long rifle, the outraged Mexicans banging away at him for all they were worth. What really riled them was that Crockett stood in plain sight as he reloaded. Yet they couldn't bring him down!

"Whyn't you fillers try grapeshot?" he called to them. "Er mebby rocks er rotten eggs?" He hunkered again, took another sight and whapped over a Mexican artilleryman. Then he stood up to reload.

It didn't take the Mexicans long to learn that the Alamo's southwest corner was a danger spot. After that, they all scattered for cover whenever they saw Crockett stand up to prime his rifle.

Santa Anna was infuriated because his snipers never hit anything. All they did was waste the general's ammo. Vindictively, he retaliated with a little psychological warfare. By the tails of Daniel's lions, he would see to it that the stupid Texans went without sleep!

The Mexican cannons roared into the night; kept it up for two hours, then shut up. And just about the time that Tack and Hank and Nap were rolling over fitfully on their cots, and Nap said, "Brother! Quiet at last!" Santa Anna's buglers cut loose with cavalry calls all around the fort. Fifteen minutes of this and ten minutes of pure silence. Then the rattle of drums; next a burst of musket fire; finally a couple hundred Mexican voices squawking, "*Viva Santa Anna!*" over and over again.

"Oh kiss my foot," Tack growled and sat up, feeling like an old crumpled newspaper someone had thrown away.

Nap grinned in the dark and propped his head on a cocked arm.

"If sleep came bottled I'd buy me a gallon of it."

"I'd give you a Mex dollar for a cupful," Tack said, smiling.

Hank sat up, looking at Tack in the gloom.

"Tack, are you still sorry you came with us?"

Tack thought about it. Well, he was still afraid; no getting around that. But was it a fear of dying or a fear of proving to be a coward? All his life, it seemed to him, he had been mentally trying to prepare himself for this one moment of courage; and yet, now that it was actually coming . . .

Suddenly he realized he was glad that he had never fallen in love: glad for the girl, whoever she might have been. Because this way he left no one behind. His mother had died when he was young. He hadn't seen his dad in two years; they hadn't got on much anyhow. He had no brothers or sisters. Every friend he had in the world—except Ben Burrows—was here in the Alamo with him.

"No," he said finally, "I guess not. I don't mind admitting I'm scared green. But no matter what happens, I think that what I've learned here will be worth it. I've learned more about life and Americans here in Texas during the last three months than I ever came close to in eighteen years on the Mississippi. I guess that's worth something."

"I guess it is," Hank said. "You know—I haven't heard you say 'It doesn't really matter, does it?' once in the last two months?"

Nap rolled over on his cot, showing them his back.

"Why don't you two deep thinkers shut up, so I can listen to Santa Anna serenade me to sleep?" he suggested.

The Mexican artillery had started again.

Tack and his two friends answered the roll call in the drizzling dawn. They felt low, and they weren't the only ones; the entire garrison seemed dispirited. This was the bad day, the day of deep-seated bitterness and unreasonable anger.

Where was Fannin, for grab's sake? And if he wasn't coming, then where were their other reinforcements? By now half of America ought to be pouring into Bexar to relieve them!

148

A day when outraged apprehension turned inward and men began to do a little soul-searching.

What am I doing here? Am I really willing to die for this old mud fort? What am I getting out of this, anyhow?

Seemingly, only Crockett's Tennesseans were unaffected by pangs of doubt. They were uncomplicated men. They knew why they were there: to shoot Mexicans. Up and down the walls they prowled, their lantern jaws swinging laterally as they worked their chaws, their eagle-sharp eyes searching for a flicker of movement among the Mexican batteries. All at once one of them would whip up his long rifle, take a casual glance along the barrel, and *whap!*

Each single shot had the instantaneous effect of an unseen hand grabbing your fiddlestring nerves—clutching them, silencing them, then letting them go, letting them throb on with life and energy.

Every time a rifleman would fire, everyone in the compound would glance up at the wall to see how he had made out. Usually they heard self-derisive comments, such as:

"Dogbone hit! Idjut Mex put his whole left arm out fum behint a log to reach him a canteen, and all I could hit was his thumb—jest behint the fust knuckle."

A distant bugle wailed. Drums rolled. Somewhere men were cheering. Hank caught Tack's arm. "Do you think it could be our reinforcements?"

Everyone in the Alamo had the same thought. Excitedly the defenders ran for the parapets and roofs and gun ramps. Tack climbed up on the artillery command post. A far-off serpent of red dust was coiling along the Larado Road, slithering into Bexar. It was the Mexicans who were doing all the cheering.

Tack spotted Lou Rose across the way on the guardhouse roof.

"Hey, Lou! What is it?"

"General Gaona, likely. I figure nigh on to 1,000 troops from all that dust they're kicking up!"

A sudden stroke of paralysis seemed to clutch at the little garrison, a momentary numbing of the will, as they stared bleakly at the dusty column filing antlike into Bexar. Gaona—Santa Anna's general.

The afternoon sun went up like a slow, serene, lemon-colored balloon and the sky was hard and clean, blue-glazed like a bowl out of a china shop. Miles Andross called to Tack, Hank and Nap to help him carry Bowie from the hospital.

Looking at the gaunt, feverish colonel, Tack didn't see how Bowie could last through the day. Sweat stood out on Bowie's face like globules of grease on a hot skillet.

"Get me out of here," he told them. "Put me in my room by the gate. I'm not going to die in any stinking hospital."

The four of them carried him cot and all into the sun-baked compound. The Alamo men stopped whatever they were doing to stare at Texas' greatest frontiersman.

"Put me down a minute," he ordered. "Tackett, prop me up where I can see the men."

Tack got an arm under the colonel's back and levered him upright. He was heavy as sin. Bowie stared at the gathering of volunteers with sick, haunted eyes.

"Colonel Travis tells me you're griping because you think Texas let you down—left you here to die. Well, who put a gun at your backs and made you come here? Nobody. You rushed here like madmen because you wanted to stop Santa Anna. Well, you're stopping him, aren't you? What more do you want—medals?"

Crockett slouched up to Bowie's cot.

"Jim, I ain't goan start frettin' about dyin' this late in the game. But Santy Anny's got 2,400 Mexes out there now, and pretty quick he's goan crush us and our matchbox fort like you'd mash a June bug with your boot. I think it'd be better ifn we was to march out and do our fightin' and dyin' in the open. I don't like to be hemmed up."

"No," Bowie said. "If we are going to die, it's important

150

that we do it in here, in this place, this Alamo. It's vital. Because we are going to give this country something it will be able to remember for a thousand years. We're going to put this place on the map." Then the old familiar fury of the violent-tempered plainsman rushed to the surface of the fever-wracked body and he shouted at them.

"What makes any of you so much better than me? If *I* can die in here, why can't you?"

Andrew Duvalt, an Irishman, cried, "Sure and what man says that Andy Duvalt won't go down by yer side, Jim me boy-o?"

The Texans started whooping, their black morning mood now abolished.

"Get me out of here," Bowie growled at Tack, "before I die right in front of them." He looked as if he were ready to do it.

The Alamo was a kind of quiet madhouse. People were penned up in its walls and they were no longer normal people, not exactly. Their stress and strain and utter exhaustion was starting to show. The endless bombardment—the cannon slam, the wail of projected shells, the gosh-awful dropping crash of the cannonballs, the whizzing fragments of shrapnel and adobe and stone—was beginning to play havoc with their nerves. They did irrational things, acted slightly abnormal.

One hour Travis issued an order that the Alamo artillery would cease fire completely to conserve on powder. The next hour he was ordering Dickinson to cut loose with the 18-pounder to show Santa Anna that they were as defiant as ever.

Tack saw Mrs. Dickinson and some of the Mexican women molding candles in cane stalks. Why? he wondered. Who's going to be here to use them?

And Lou Rose had changed. He seemed to shun the company of others, wouldn't talk to anyone. Tack found him hunkering in the shade of the north postern gun ramp.

"What's eating you, Lou? Hardly ever see you anymore."

"So I want to be alone! Something wrong in that?"

"No, but if you've got problems, maybe I can help with 'em."

"You! I thought you was the boy who was scared to death to come to Texas."

"Well, yeah," Tack admitted. "But Colonel Bowie said—"

"Hang Bowie! He's gonna die anyhow, and he knows it. So what loss is it to him to stay here? But you 'n' me, Tack, we ain't dying of any disease. So I say—" Rose broke off, glancing at Tack covertly, then sideslipped his eyes.

"What? What are you trying to say?"

"Nothin'," Rose muttered bearishly. "Just lemme alone, huh?"

"All right, Lou," Tack said. He started away. Then he looked back. Lou Rose was staring after him with a peculiar expression.

Night came like the dropping of a spangled cloak, and with it a blank stillness. But not for long. Santa Anna's serenade started, then stopped—to usher in another expectant stillness. It went on that way all night long: each blank space of silence suddenly ripped to shreds by a gut-grabbing bugle call, or a cannon blast from the gun emplacement in the torn-down district of La Villita, or a musket volley from the burrows the Mexicans had dug along the riverbank; while up on the walls, the never-needing-to-sleep Tennesseans were answering the serenade with occasional rifle fire, calling advice and information and insults to one another far into the night.

Pak!

"I be liced! Mex observer jest went to stick his eyes overn the top of a embankment to take him a peek at us. Pore fool never stopped to think they was a cookfire right

152

behint him. Think he'd know better'n thet—and him only 170 yards away!"

"Wal, instead a tellin' us all about his life history—did you git him?"

"Oh not so you'd notice. Jest parted his hair some—the hair on his eyebrows is all."

That night another batch of "friendly" Mexicans deserted the Alamo and slipped into Bexar. One of them was a woman and she went right to the Yturri House and demanded to see *El Presidente*.

"The walls of the Alamo are crumbling from your cannon fire, General," she informed Santa Anna. "Their ammunition and food is low, and the men are weak. Your army could take the fort in a minute!"

Santa Anna had just put the finishing touches to a dispatch to Mexico City. The message reported his brilliant (and Napoleonic) capture of the town of Bexar. He had not mentioned *one word* about the 186 adamant Texans who were still making their defiant stand in the Alamo!

He listened to the Mexican woman with avid interest and then hurried her out of headquarters with a mumbled *Muchas gracias*. He called in Generals Sesma, Gaona, Cós, Amador and Castrillón for a council of war. It was short and sweet and not one of the generals had a chance to open his mouth or to offer a word of advice.

"*Caballeros,*" Santa Anna announced, putting one hand into his silver-frogged jacket front. "We are going to attack!"

14

ANYBODY KIN STEP ACROST A
LI'L OLD LINE IN THE DIRT

It was morning, March 3.

A scattering of musket shots caromed out of the hills. A sentry on the church ramp yelled, "Rider comin'! Hell fer leather!"

The garrison, stupid with sleep (or lack of it), rushed to the walls and watched a lone rider come piling down from Powder House Hill. He came as if the Three Furies were harping on his nag's flowing tail. It was Bonham.

He rode low in the saddle, hunched over, and he kept murmuring *Go it! Go it!* in his big sorrel's right ear, putting the horse into the first spread of fields. Then he was out in the open and over the field and he looked across the clearing to where a ragged rumple in the field marked Sesma's battery. Behind the embankment were the snouts of Sesma's guns and one of them flashed a spark like a flash of light in a mirror and the oncoming shell ripped the fabric of the dawn sky with a gaudy wail and Bonham and his horse both felt the slap of cushioned air rush by them.

The dirt of the earth spouted upward in a cloddy fountain 25 yards beyond the sorrel's nigh side and Bonham said, "Come on, you big red Mex *caballo*," and the sorrel seemed to understand the urging, or maybe the fear of shell-screaming was in him, because he suddenly broke loose with everything his forearms and gaskins had, the coronets of his hoofs rising and blurring with the smooth rapid pace of his galloping rhythm, and Bonham could feel the tensing heave of the horse's ribs and the thrusting chopping drive of his legs.

Then the La Villita battery opened up on Bonham's left, and as quick as he saw the glint-glint-glint of the flashes he started to seesaw the sorrel's head and they went into a forward-going zigzag and the field mushroomed dirt and clods and weeds all around them.

Now the dun-colored walls of the Alamo lunged before him and he put the horse at the stockaded outworks, seeing the gate flying open and seeing Crockett and the kid called Tackett and a few others running out to cover his entry with their rifles. He sawed the sorrel's head and they swerved as one into the outworks, sawed again, swerved again, and the sorrel went pounding through the gate.

Tack dropped to his left knee and blasted at a chasing troop of Mexican dragoons with his shotgun—even though they were yards out of range. Then Crockett hit him on the shoulder.

"C'mon! You heerd what Bowie said: no dyin' out in the open!"

Tack grinned and he and the rest darted back to the outworks and into the Alamo. Bonham was dismounting, and Travis was at his side. No, Bonham said, no reinforcements. He had been to Goliad and to Gonzales. Doc Sutherland and Captain Seguin were supposed to be on their way with some volunteers, but exactly where they were no one knew for sure.

Surprisingly enough the garrison was not discouraged by Bonham's news. They had long ago given up Fannin anyhow. Now, in their almost fanatical diehard abnormal attitude, they were welded together in purpose. They understood the importance of holding the Alamo—not only as a strategic military position, but as a symbol of Texas determination as well.

Travis noticed Tack in the compound and called him over.

"I'm going to send a final message, Tackett. If you take it, and *if* you break through the enemy's lines, you will probably live to a ripe old age. Do you want to go?"

Tack thought about it for a moment, then shook his head.

"I think I'd rather stay here with my friends, Colonel."

Funny, the moment he said it he knew he was signing his own death warrant. Well—it didn't really matter, did it?

Travis called for the old frontiersman John Smith. He wrote two final letters. Neither of them were appeals for help. The first was a public message to Washington-on-the-Brazos. The second was a private message to David Ayers who was keeping Travis' little son, Charles:

> Take care of my little boy. If the country should be saved, I may make him a splendid fortune; but if the country should be lost and I should perish, he will have nothing but the proud recollection that he is the son of a man who died for his country.

Some of the defenders decided to pen a few hurried lines to parents, wives, sweethearts and friends; Hank for one, Tack for another. Nap just grinned. No one was waiting for him at home. Tack decided to write to old Ben Burrows.

> You've probably never heard of this place—I sure hadn't 3 months ago. Anyhow, we've committed ourselves to fighting the Mexicans to the last man. So I don't think I'll see you or the old Miss again. Do me a favor, Ben, look up my dad next time you're in New Orleans. He's a wealthy lonely widower and he's prob-

ably wondering whatever became of his only son. We never understood each other, but tell him for me that I didn't turn out too bad after all. . . .

He gave his letter to old man Smith.

"Whyn't you come with me?" Smith asked. "Travis'd let you."

Tack shook his head. "I have friends here."

Jerry Day, a Missouri boy, led a party of skirmishers through the sally port in the north postern. It was black midnight and they started firing blind in the general direction of Sesma's battery. The Mexicans got all panicky about it and opened up with their heavy guns and then sent an infantry patrol forward to repel the supposed attack.

Under this created diversion, John Smith charged through the main gate on a tall strong horse and was long gone in the night.

Morning, March 4th. The sun strutted over the eastern hills like a knight in burnished armor, gold-plated and brilliant with the confidence of great power.

Santa Anna's bombardment pressed closer and closer, the shells pounding the old walls into near rubble. The Alamo's sharpshooters cracked back at them. It was a long, hot, powder-stained day. Crockett made numerous trips to his quarters to visit a friendly jug he had stashed there. Once he paused to make an entry in his journal:

> Pop, pop, pop! Bom, bom, bom! throughout the day. No time for memorandums now. Go ahead! Liberty and independence forever!

Those were the last written words to come from Davy Crockett.

Morning, March 5th.

From the hospital roof Tack observed ominous signs of activity in the ruins of La Villita. The Mexican infantrymen were busy as beavers slapping together ladders—scaling ladders.

Suddenly it seemed inconceivable to him that the time he had secretly feared for so long—*la Hora de la Verdad*—was at hand. Always it had seemed to him to belong in the vague future of next month, next week, the day after tomorrow. And all at once he realized that the time was now. Next month, next week, the day after tomorrow was here!

An abrupt and overwhelming horror of pain and death struck him and he started back from the parapet as if propelled by a physical blow. Instantly the alluring temptations of escape from the net that was drawing closer in with every passing hour flooded his harassed mind.

There had to be a way out! He had to find it and take it! This very minute! Now. . . .

He sensed a change in his surroundings. His panic suspended and he paused to look around, wondering. Then he realized what it was. Stillness. Santa Anna's bombardment had ceased. All the Mexican batteries were mysteriously mute.

The garrison reacted the same as Tack—puzzled. What did it mean? Tack saw Travis walk across the compound and go up the ramp to the 18-pounder. A minute later the colonel returned to the Plaza and called the garrison to gather around him.

Tack hurried down from the roof and pushed through the Texans until he found Hank.

"Men," Travis addressed them, "I believe there can be only one reason for this sudden lull. Santa Anna is preparing to attack." He paused as though selecting his next words with care.

"Courageous men fight best when they have no illusions. So I'm telling you quite frankly that our position here is desperate. We can no longer hope for outside help. It simply isn't coming. So we have three choices: surrender unconditionally, try to escape, or make a stand and fight to the last man." He paused again, staring at his dusty boots. He suddenly looked old.

"If we make a stand, we are doing it not so much for Houston—who desperately needs the time, Lord knows—but rather for Texas. What we do in this place will give Texas a backbone on which to grow. Speaking for myself—I'm staying. But I won't force any man to stay with me. The choice must be your own."

He drew his sword and made a long line in the ground with the point of the blade.

"I want every man who is willing to stay with me to declare his intention by crossing over this line."

Crockett shouldered his rifle and strode forward.

"Shucks, Colonel, I thought you was fixin' to ask us to do somethin' hard. Anybody kin step acrost a li'l old line in the dirt!"

Hank started forward, then looked back at Tack. Nap shuffled by them, grinning about it. A line, a river, he didn't care what he crossed. It was all a big game to him. Richard Allen cleared his throat self-consciously and walked toward the line. Now more and more of them were doing it: Richardson Perry, Robert Brown, David Cummings, Galba Fuqua and Johnny Gaston, both sixteen years old, the three Taylor brothers from Liberty, Texas, Asa Walker, old Tom Hendricks . . .

A cluster of men came from Bowie's room. They were bearing the sick colonel on his cot. Bowie raised his head and nodded.

"Set me down on the other side of the line," he said.

Tack realized that Hank was still watching him, still waiting. He smiled sheepishly and walked toward his friend.

"Couldn't seem to get my feet started for a second there," he said.

Hank laughed and slapped him on the back. They went over the line together.

Tack didn't know why, but he felt good—so good his eyes grew moist. He grinned impulsively and looked around at all his friends. Then he stopped grinning and looked again.

One lone man was standing in the Plaza on the other side of the line, standing there with a sort of defiant hang-dog expression on his tough face.

Lou Rose.

"You'll never even git over them walls, son," Crockett said to Lou Rose. He and Rose, Tack and Hank were standing around Bowie's cot. The rest of the garrison had gone back to their posts in disgust. "The Mexes will snipe you cold."

Rose squinted up at the Alamo's staunch walls.

"I've climbed worse'n them under fire in my time," he muttered.

"Don't do it, Lou," Bowie said weakly. "Stay with us. You belong here. We all do. We've earned this place."

"Well, you can have my share of it and welcome!" Rose cried. "Why *should* I stay? What's it going to get me except an early death? Man can't make any money dyin' like a dog in here."

"There's more to war than money," Bowie whispered.

"Yeah? What?" Rose demanded. "Glory? Huh! Money's the only thing I ever fought for. I'm a professional soldier. Glory don't buy any beans—just an unmarked grave in a battlefield. You been fightin' for glory all your life, Colonel, and what's it ever got you? Here you are dying, and you're broke."

Bowie was quiet for a moment, then he said, "Sure, money's a good thing. But there's something you can say for glory that you can't say for money. You can take glory with you, when it's your time to go."

It was night and Tack was leaning on the parapet of the

160

northeast angle, staring absently at the silent roar of the black vastness of space which stretched around the Alamo.

He was thinking of the Mississippi, seeing again the great steamboats marching grandly down the river, tall and square and gleaming white in the sun, with their black-snake banners of smoke coiling overhead. He wondered how old Ben was getting along, and how Fanny Preston had made out with her highwayman.

Someone was coming quietly along the wall toward him. It was Lou Rose, carrying the shotgun Crockett had given him in Alexandria.

"Let's get out of here, Tack," Rose muttered. "You don't want to stay in this rabbit box any more'n I do."

"Are you really going to desert, Lou?"

"Bet your sweet life on it! Think I'm stupid? What do you say?"

Tack rubbed at his mouth, then shook his head.

"No. Bowie's right. We belong here."

"In a pig's tail we do! Maybe Nap does, because he ain't got the sense God give a flea. And maybe Hank does, too, because he's one of them glory boys that believes in fighting for a lost cause."

"But it's *not* a lost cause, Lou. It's just starting, and we're going to win. I can feel it, somehow."

Rose snorted. "All you're going to feel is a Mex bayonet."

"Lou, I was just now thinking of the Mississippi. Remember what we said that day on the keelboat? That we would all stick together, the four of us?"

"Well, it don't really matter, does it?"

"It *does* matter! Can't you see that if we back down here, then we'll always back down? Then Texas will remain under the rule of that Mexican madman. But there's more than Texas' liberty at stake. All of us so-called Texans are really Americans. There's only about twenty-five actual Texans in the Alamo. And if we surrender or pack up and crawl home, then we're doing it as Americans and America will stand disgraced. World opinion will point its finger at us and say, 'There go the gutless Americans. Boy, have *they* changed since their War of Independence.' "

Rose was staring at him blankly.

"I guess I had you figured wrong all along, Tack. I thought you was chickenhearted. But you ain't. You're just plain stupid like Hank. Well, there's no sense in arguing about it. I'm a professional soldier. I know when it's time to attack and when it's time to retreat. That's the trouble with this bunch in here: 184 men and not one of 'em a real soldier, except me. Well—" He hesitated, then thrust the shotgun at Tack.

"Here, give it back to Crockett. Nobody can say I took something that wasn't mine." He put his hands on the parapet.

"Lou," Tack said. "I've never completely trusted you, but I've always admired you because I knew you were a real soldier. I've even defended you against the others, made excuses for your behavior. Well, I don't admire you anymore. Because you're a stupid little man, Lou. Because you can't see tomorrow for worrying about today. Because you—"

"Shut up!" Lou hissed. "Shut up or I'll run this Elgin in you!"

"Try it. C'mon, soldier of fortune, try it. What have *I* got to lose?"

Rose stalled, caught between anger—and what? Friendship? He relaxed, put away the Elgin pistol. "So long, kid," he muttered. He swung himself over the parapet and dropped into the night.

He had chosen the right time for it. The night was a blind universe and the black fields seemed to be deserted. He crawled down to the creek and followed it north, sticking in the shelter of the tules. Then he cut to the east, into the fallow fields again, and approached the gloomy hills.

An hour later he paused at the mouth of a dry gulch and looked back at the distant blocky silhouette of the old Alamo.

"Suckers," he whispered. He went on down the gulch and out of history.

The *Degüello*

15

FROM NOW ON HIT'S EVERY
MAN FOR HIMSELF

It was 4:30 A.M. the morning of March 6.

Santa Anna had slung 1,800 Mexicans around the brooding Alamo. They were moving through the dark weeds quietly, cautiously, slowly tightening their circle.

As usual General Santa Anna had done everything himself—had made all the plans, all the arrangements, had thought of every little detail right down to the last bandage and bullet. The plan of attack was his special pride and joy. . . .

Cós would hit the northwest corner with scaling ladders; Duque would strike the northeast with grenadiers; Romero would overthrow Crockett's palisade in the east; Morales would charge the main gate in the south, and Sesma's dragoons would back up Romero in the east.

Perfect! Beautiful! *Bueno* for the great general! Napoleon himself couldn't have planned the attack better.

Santa Anna stood on a little hill in the north with 600 men held in reserve. His bugler stood at his side, licking his lips nervously, waiting for the general's command to announce the grand attack.

Santa Anna rubbed his hands excitedly and glanced toward the east. It was now 4:45 and still no hint of the dawn in the dark cloud-mottled sky. The tension was mounting, everyone could feel it. They wanted something to happen, anything, just to put an end to this apprehensive waiting.

5:00 A.M. How much longer?

Suddenly the strain became too much for one of the Mexican soldiers. He let out a nervous yell.

"*Viva Santa Anna!*"

Santa Anna was stunned by the unexpected cry.

"Herod's great-aunt and lame godfather! What fool was that?" he raged.

Now more and more troops began shouting the *vivas* and all at once it seemed as if *every* Mexican in the weeds was yelling and cheering.

Nombre d'un Nombre! Why, *why* did something *always* have to go wrong? Santa Anna nodded to the bugler and the man stepped forward and made a blaring flourish with his bugle, the notes racing clean and shrill into the cloud-hung dark.

All around the Alamo Mexican bugles began firing strident calls, and the officers yelled, "*Arriba! Arriba! Muchachos!*" as the emotionally pent-up troops sprang from the weeds and started their rush on the fort.

"The Mexicans are coming! Fall out! Fall out!" the Alamo sentries cried, and started firing into the tremulous dark.

Tack, Hank, Nap and others rolled from their cots in the long barracks and grabbed boots, guns and ammo pouches. Nap grinned back as he started for the door.

165

"See you boys later—when we line up for our medals in heaven!"

It was the last time Tack ever saw him. He felt Hank's hand grip his shoulder.

"Luck, Tack!"

"Same to you, Hank!"

Seemed funny to Tack that in stories—at this tense moment—there always seemed to be ample time for the characters to reassure one another of their devotion; oceans of time in which they could remind each other of what grand times they had had together. But it wasn't true. They didn't have a spare second. Just a quick reluctant word. That's all the time there was.

Tack darted through the door, collided with someone (Charles Zanco from Denmark, he thought) in the dark, and ran to the first ladder. He scrambled up to the parapet on the long barracks. Men were aligned on either side of him, stretching off into the rifle-flashing darkness. They each had four-five loaded rifles leaning against the parapet and they went *bap . . . bap . . . bap* at Romero's troops like a man driving a nail with a hammer.

Colonel Romero had gotten himself all bollixed up. His troops had started for the palisade but became confused when they reached the creek—nor had Crockett's handy sharpshooters helped them much at straightening themselves out. First thing Romero knew, his men were charging in the wrong direction, surging for the corrals and toward Colonel Duque's column.

Now the Alamo's 12-pounders belched into action, and the artillerymen and riflemen were firing at such a terrific rate that it looked to Tack as if the whole Alamo was bathed in a blazing, spastic light.

The Mexicans waded doggedly on through the lead storm, faltering, stumbling, falling. General Cós' column was stopped cold by cannon fire, and blast after blast of langrage, canister and grape went plowing into Duque's men, forty troops going down at one toss, and Colonel Duque himself hit the ground with a shattered kneecap as his combat-crazy troops came boot-clomping right on over him, mashing him into the weeds and dirt just as if he was a nobody.

Tack stepped back to reload his shotgun and glanced down into the compound. He saw Travis running across the light-flickering Plaza with the Negro Joe at his heels.

Travis ran up to the gun platform on the north wall and fired his double-barreled shotgun over the parapet, yelling, "C'mon, boys! Blast 'em!"

For a moment he looked like a demon, silhouetted in the flash fire and in the eerie glow of the Mexican rockets which climbed the dusky sky.

Disorganized clumps of Cós' and Duque's men had reached the trenches beneath the walls and Travis saw them struggling down there in the dark.

"No surrender! No surrender, *muchachos!*" he roared, and he raised his shotgun and voiced a cry to the Texans which would later become famous to all Yankees in another war.

"Hurrah, my boys! Hurrah!"

A spiteful volley flared from the scrambled Mexicans in the ditch and Travis reeled back dropping his gun, clamped his hands to his head and took a blind step into nothing, his outthrust foot missing the ramp by inches. He plunged into the compound, into the flashing shadows, rolled partway upright and sagged against the log foot of the ramp.

Joe came leaping down to Travis' side. He bent over Travis, caught him by the shoulders, and then straightened up shaking his burr head. He started backing away. Suddenly he turned and ran into the barracks.

Tack rubbed at his mouth and sprang to the ladder, tumbled down the rungs and raced across the yard to

167

Travis' huddled form. The colonel wasn't dead, he saw, but he was the next thing to it. He had been hit in the head and he was dying in a stunned daze.

Tack looked up at the walls. The Texans were cheering!

"What's happened?" he called to Captain Baugh, the adjutant.

"They're retreating! We beat 'em off! Tell the colonel they're regrouping for another attack!"

Tell the colonel. . . . Tack looked at Travis, at the body that had been Colonel William Barret Travis. He started across the compound at a run, all the way across, into Colonel Bowie's room just left of the main gate.

Bowie was up on one elbow in his cot and, in the fluttery light of a single candle, he looked worse than the last rose of summer.

"What's happening?" he demanded hoarsely.

"We beat off their first attack, sir. But they're regrouping for another. Colonel Travis is dead."

Bowie wet his lips and made a gesture with his hand.

"Move the table with that candle over by the door. Get me those two pistols from that hutch, and my knife."

Tack jockeyed the table to one side of the door and fetched the colonel his set of long-barreled dueling pistols. Then he drew the long-bladed knife from its buckskin sheath.

The great bowie knife . . . the most famous knife in history.

"Prop me up," Bowie ordered, and Tack heaved the gaunt man upright in his cot. Bowie arranged his weapons just so on top of his blanket. Pistols to the right, knife to the left. He looked at Tack.

"Still scared?"

"Yes, sir!"

Bowie grinned. "Me too. But we're lucky. It could've been Comanches. One thing I can promise you. When

Santa Anna does it to you, it comes fast. He doesn't play around with it. That make you feel better?"

Tack managed to grin. "No, sir."

Bowie coughed a gargled laugh. "Go tell that 'high private' Crockett that I've promoted him. He's in command now."

Tack started for the door but was arrested in mid-stride by the sudden heart-clutching wail of strange music.

"What's that?"

"That?" Bowie said wryly. "That's the *Degüello*, the Mexican army's battle hymn. Means the same thing as their red flag—no quarter, no mercy. Weird sound, eh?"

Doo-oom — da-dat-dat — doo-oomm — da-dat-dat — doo-oommm . . .

Doom, Tack thought bleakly. "Good luck, Colonel," he said.

"Fresh out of it," Bowie said.

Crockett's Tennesseans were reloading their multitude of rifles and the colonel himself was expounding his Washington departure to Hank Warnell.

"So I said to my Washington constituents (which, I've heered, is a Shawnee word meanin' polecat), 'You go to—' "

And Hank was standing there smiling, just as if he'd never heard the to-hell-and-Texas story before.

"Colonel," Tack interposed. "Colonel Bowie says you are to assume command. Colonel Travis is dead."

"He is, eh?" Crockett spat and rubbed at his ear. "That's too bad. I never thought much a Travis, I reckon. A lee-tle too high-toned fer my blood. But he was a brimstone-eater of a soldier! Dandy ways 'n' all. Well! The only order I got to give as garrison commander is this: From now on hit's every man for himself! Lay hit on, boys!"

Tack waved to Hank and started back toward the Plaza.

He saw old Tom Hendricks sitting with his back to the stubby adobe wall that separated the chapel yard from the Plaza. Tom was nursing a winged left arm with a strip of linen from a Mexican woman's petticoat. He had a little cluster of grenades piled next to him.

"You all right, Tom?"

"Wal, don't I look all right? Shore I be. Jest got me a bit of a beesting here. But they's nuthin' a-tall wrong with my slingin' arm!" He patted his pile of grenades with his right hand.

"You have a punk for those grenades?" Tack asked.

"Uh-uh. Got me a see-gar. That colored boy Joe fetched hit to me. Funny fella. Says he's only twenty-three but he looks twice thet age. Reckon he's had him a rough life."

"Reckon he has," Tack said. "See you, Tom."

"Soon!" old Tom called after him.

Too soon, Tack thought, knowing that he and Tom were both thinking of the same thing.

General Antonio López de Santa Anna was methodically plucking one frothy plume after another from his elegant hat, like a lovelorn schoolboy: She loves me, she loves me not—they'll fight me, they'll fight me not. He threw his hat to the ground.

"Attack! Attack! Attack!" he raged.

The battered Mexican army—the bugles blaring, the drums rolling, the *Degüello* dooom-ing—charged again.

Tack gained the parapet on the long barracks roof and looked out at the battle-scarred fields. The sun, colored like the meat of a ripe plum, was just starting on the eastern horizon. *My last sunrise*, he suddenly thought. But there was no time to reflect upon it; not even enough time to remember that he was afraid.

The four Mexican columns rushed forward again, more or less in their original order of battle, which (like most planned battles) looked excellent on paper, but which

170

didn't quite pan out when it came down to the individual combat soldier—who was, after all, nothing more than a frightened, confused human being.

Bonham was up on the church platform and he opened the proceedings with a roar of 12-pounders. Then the Texans on top of the long barracks cut loose with their rifles and the north and west and south walls blasted forth a hail of scrap iron.

The Mexicans drop-drop-dropped. They couldn't seem to wade through the murderous Alamo fire. Individuals, parts of squads, half a platoon, would wedge themselves up to the ditches—where the grape-spewing cannons roared harmlessly overhead—only to find themselves caught in the sights of the Texas riflemen.

All along the walls the rifles went *WHOW WHOW WHOW* throwing flashes of orange into the dark.

Tack fired right barrel, left barrel, and stepped back and reloaded in a hysteria of haste and stepped up again and aimed and fired right, left, the spastic jolt of the butt kicking solidly in his shoulder, and seeing Mexicans go down in a thrash of weeds, and not only Mexicans now, because Texans were spinning around and dropping, too.

Richardson Perry fell and his legs kicked even after he was dead and his fingers went twitch, twitch. . . .

Sixteen-year-old Galba Fuqua came stumbling down the ramp in the church nave. He was clutching his shattered lower jaw and he looked at Mrs. Dickinson who was huddled in the sacristy with her infant daughter. He said, "Ga-a-uh-vexicans—"

"I can't understand you!" Mrs. Dickinson cried. "Is my husband all right?"

Fuqua grabbed at his splintered jaw and tried to work out his words manually. But they were only garbled sounds. He shrugged and ran back up the ramp to the roof, to continue the fight.

The Mexican charge—all four prongs—fell back for the

171

second time in great disorder. Santa Anna gave his hat a good lick with his boot and called upon Moses and some of his lesser relatives and screamed loud and long for a third attack.

This time everything that could go wrong *did* go wrong.

Once again Colonel Romero's men swept away from the withering fire of the palisade and the church and went reeling through the lead holocaust from the long barracks and blundered headlong into the Duque column.

At the same time, baffled by the slashing grape, General Cós' troops surged to the east and they too stumbled into Duque's column. The result was that a great tumble of bewildered men struck the north wall all at once.

Talk about chaos! The scaling ladders were lost under the falling piles of dead and wounded, infantry hopelessly mixed with plunging cavalry, grenades landing among the tangled clots of troops, the Texas rifles going *whap whap whap* into the scrambling melee. . . .

Santa Anna picked up his battered hat and idly started plucking plumes from it once again. He felt sick. He felt like Napoleon at Waterloo. All his beautiful plans and arrangements. And now look at what his idiot officers and troops were doing. Just look!

Screaming like a disturbed squawk heron in a swamp, Santa Anna ordered his reserves forward.

Tack found himself caught in a yelling, surging rush toward the north wall. The Mexicans kept piling up at the northeast angle of the fort. Shouting and scrambling and rearing upward, they were finding hand- and footholds in the cannon-breached walls. But the Texans were above— firing into the jammed pack, flailing their rifle butts, driving home hunting knives, slashing with swords, knocking the scrabbling Mexicans from the walls like so many ants.

General Cós ordered his troops out of the squirming mess, directing them to swing around and charge the

Alamo's west wall. He had spotted a few breach spots there. . . .

And now Morales' troops started to gang up at the corner where the 18-pounder still roared defiance at the dawn.

They were making it. All at once it started to go their way. From three different points the Mexicans were piling helter-skelter over the parapets; 1,500 of them clamoring and clawing and sprawling over the walls, through the breaches and into the Alamo.

Tack, on the roof of the artillery barracks, pulled back from the brawl, reloading his shotgun as hurriedly as his trembling fingers would work. Someone, somewhere, was yelling in English:

"Form in the compound! Fall back in the long barracks!"

Uh-uh, he wasn't having any of that. Days ago Travis had barricaded all the doors and archways in the long barracks with hide sandbags; but Tack didn't want to be caught in that kind of trap.

He looked around wildly, seeing everywhere the disorganized jumbles of Mexicans boiling into the fort, and he started running for the long barracks roof. He scrambled onto the roof, crawled over Richardson Perry's stiffening body, and glanced into the Plaza.

Texas gunners had fallen back to the elevated cannons in the compound and were blasting away at the tangle of Mexicans pouring over the northeast wall. But not for long. Morales' troops came surging over the south wall and down the ramp and charged the compound guns with their glittering bayonets.

Tack picked up Perry's rifle and someone else's ammo pouch, and headed for home—his favorite position in the Alamo, the hospital roof. He would make his lone stand there. His last stand.

173

16

IT REALLY DID MATTER AFTER
ALL, DIDN'T IT?

Captain Dickinson ran into the darkened church sacristy, crying:

"Sue, the Mexicans are inside our walls!"

He only had a moment to wrap his arms around his shivering, speechless wife, then Bonham—stripped to the waist, his face and chest powder-stained (truly the Black Knight now)—shouted down at him.

"C'mon, Dickinson! Let's hold the church!"

"Save the child, if they spare you!" Dickinson said to his wife. Then he was gone and she never saw him again.

An Irishman, Bill Ward, worked the cannon in the Plaza until the last minute. Tom Hendricks, still sitting with his back to the stubby adobe wall, watched Ward disappear under a picket-fencelike charge of bayonets. *My turn next,* Tom thought.

He took a deep drag on his cigar, touched the glowing

174

end to a grenade fuse and lobbed the heavy iron object at the first mob of Mexicans that started toward him.

The grenade went off with a *KA-PLOWM* scattering Mexicans and parts of Mexicans over the yard. Old Tom grinned and reached for his second grenade as another gang of Mexicans rushed at him, firing their English Waterloo muskets as they ran.

He got the fuse going just as a bullet plunked in his chest.

"*Uuah!*" he grunted, doubling half over. Then he straightened up, the sparking grenade in his right hand.

"Know what Arnold would've thought of you?" he yelled at them. "*This!*"

His right hand went back but he didn't lob the bomb. He let it go off above his head as three of the Mexicans came driving in with their bayonets.

Tom went to glory with company.

Mrs. Alsbury and her sister Gertrudis were huddled in a little room next to the Alamo headquarters. Afraid that the Mexicans might peg a grenade into the room, Gertrudis threw open the door and started to yell.

"Don't fire! There's only women in here!"

A Mexican soldier slammed to a halt and made a grab at her. Gertrudis drew back to Mrs. Alsbury's side in terror, and the soldier followed her into the room. He was grinning from ear to ear.

He wasn't the only one who could grin. Nap Mitchell sprang through the doorway with a hunting knife in his hand.

"*Adiós, amigo!*" he said, and he punched the knife home as the Mexican spun about.

Still grinning, Nap blinked at Mrs. Alsbury as she let out a scream and pointed over his shoulder. He started to pivot. . . .

Nap never knew it was a bayonet that caught him in the back.

Jim Bowie pulled himself into a sitting position, thinking, *Let them come soon now—before I fall over. Let 'em come while I'm at least sitting up, not lying down like a dying dog.*

He picked up his dueling pistols and cocked the locks, liking the smooth, oiled, double-jointed *co-lok-lok* feel of their movement. He sat there dazedly, waiting, as the tumultuous sounds of the hand-to-hand fighting drew closer and closer, and he thought about the Creole dandy who had once slapped his face and challenged him to a duel. . . .

"You're mad if you accept," his friends had told him. "That Creole is a past master at both the pistol and the sword."

But Bowie had grinned because, as the man who had been challenged, the choice of weapons and the rules of the duel were his privilege.

Cutlasses, he had told the Creole's seconds, and they had smiled, thinking that Bowie had just signed his own death warrant.

In a locked dark room, he had added.

According to the conventions of dueling, Bowie had been authorized to call the play. The Creole was honor-bound not to object. They had been put into a locked, windowless, dark room, each with a naked cutlass in his hand. . . .

Bowie's mouth twisted into a sick smile. So, here he was waiting for the Mexicans to find him in this room. And the Creole? Well, Mexicans were one thing that Creole would never have to worry about.

The door to his room reverberated under the blows of a musket butt. It sprang open, jolting on its frame, and the first Mexican infantryman came driving in with his bayonet and somersaulted to the floor as Bowie's right pistol went *POWM*, and then the second soldier darted in, trying to weave from side to side, but got bollixed up with the dead one's outflung legs, and Bowie's left pistol piled him into a clump.

Bowie set down his empty pistols and reached for his old friend—the long, single-edged, taper-nosed knife—and shoved himself up from the cot with his left hand as the third and fourth and fifth Mexican rushed him.

He struck the first bayonet aside with the great knife, yelling, *EEE-YAH!* and waded in, planting the blade just as he had done long ago in the famous Sand Bar Fight. Then he let that man and the knife go and grabbed for the fourth one with his left hand, getting a clutch on the squirming, screaming Mexican's neck.

And after that it didn't really matter what they did to him with their bayonets because he had that man and no one, nothing, could ever make Jim Bowie let go.

Some of the defenders had had enough. A handful of Texans leaped over the palisade to make a break into the open. This is what Sesma's cavalry had been waiting for. They rolled forward on their plunging mounts and hacked down the runaways with sabers, speared them with lances. One Texan got as far as the footbridge. Then they caught him, shot him as he lurked under the bridge.

But these were only a few. Crockett and the Tennesseans —fighting at bay in the chapel yard—weren't about to run. The Mexicans tore into the palisade, ripping open breaches, toppling whole sections of pales at a time. And if they thought Texans were tough fighters, then the Tennessee boys had news for them.

With rifle fire, hunting knives, gun butts, rocks and fists, the Tennesseans became wildcats. They beat the Mexicans back, down and under. They war-whooped and cussed, and when they were hit and fell to the ground they died the hard way—still reaching around for a gun or a knife or a rock, still cussing.

Sam Blair clutched a wounded Mexican in the crook of his mighty left arm and held the senseless man in front of him as a shield, while his right hand went *WHOW WHOW WHOW* with a .44 pistol, blasting apart a frantic rush of Mexicans, and he was doing fine, just fine, until one of Santa Anna's *Zapadores* slipped around behind him with a sword. . . .

Hank Warnell had picked up a *Zapadore*'s sword and now found himself facing Tack's old shadow, Sergeant Felix Nuñez. Hank knew nothing about swordplay. He fought like an Arab—hack and slash. But Nuñez was an old cavalryman and a sword was like the extension of his right arm.

He warded off a couple of Hank's wild blows and set himself, waiting his turn, and the next time Hank swung up his sword to aim a chopping blow, Nuñez darted forward— under and in with the point of his blade.

Hank felt the quick stab of pain in the right side of his chest—so hot and hard and sudden it burned like a splinter of ice. He reeled back, his left heel striking the dirt embankment at the foot of the palisade, and for a vivid moment it seemed that an entire section of pales was crashing down on him.

Richard Allen was in the long barracks behind the sandbag barricades. He had no idea how many Texans were in the other dark, loopholed rooms, and it didn't really matter to him. His entire being was now concentrated on one purpose: to make the Mexicans pay dearly for his life.

He had gathered up four or five rifles and he worked them furiously, panning and firing through a loophole at the torrent of confused Mexicans racing this way and that across the cluttered Plaza. Nearly ninety other Texans were doing the same thing—bowling over running Mexicans right and left.

General Amador on the north wall, and Colonel Morales on the south, realized that this sort of nonsense would have to be eliminated immediately. Think of the troops these wildcat Texans had already cost Santa Anna's army!

They gave hasty orders to swing around the 18-pounder on the south wall and the two 12-pounders on the north and open fire. The three cannons roared point-blank at the long barracks, again and again and again. As from far away, Allen sensed cascades of blinding, rending light coming for him. All the fires in the world leaped at him. Abruptly, they went out, forever.

Tack wiped his face and looked around. He was alone on the hospital roof. Dawn was coming for him like a golden promise. Too soon, he thought emptily. Yes, much too soon.

The Mexican band was still *dooom*-ing the air with the *Degüello*.

Below him, the Texans died the way soldiers always died —screaming and cursing and kicking around. He checked his arms. He had three rifles and his shotgun but he was short on ammo, mighty short. Down on the roof of the long barracks lay three dead Mexican sergeants. They had tried to lower the blue silk flag of the New Orleans Greys, the Alamo's only banner. Now a lieutenant was scrambling over the parapet to have a try. Tack raised a rifle.

It was Lieutenant José María Torres and he was carrying the red, white and green Mexican colors under his arm. A Lieutenant Martinez was with him.

Martinez yanked down the Alamo flag and opened his mouth to give a victory shout. *POW!* He fell, wearing the flag like a cloak. Torres quickly ran up the Mexican colors as Tack swung up another rifle. Funny way to repay a man who once more or less saved your life, but then war was a funny game. . . .

He shot Torres dead. He reloaded all his weapons and moved hurriedly around the parapets, staring into the battle-littered Plaza and yards below.

It was as good as over, of course. The Texans had lost the walls, the Plaza and the long barracks. The Mexicans were now mopping up the great compound, firing volley after volley into the darkened rooms. Tack recognized Robert Brown's body by the well, bayoneted. Then he looked into the chapel yard and saw a sight which made him wish that he could live a long, long time, if only to remember it.

Crockett was the last Tennessean on his feet. He had his back to the high corral wall and he had a stand of rifles at his side. A messy half-moon of dead and wounded Mexicans sprawled in front of him, and as more and more Mexicans came piling through the broken palisade, Crockett would whip up a rifle and go *bap*, grab for another and *bap* again, and then another . . . and the Mexicans blasted back at him, point-blank, and missed him time and again, and kept trying to get at him with their bayonets like a pack of fang-bared wolves snapping at a lone shaggy bear.

Then his rifles were empty and he grabbed one by the barrel and started swinging the gunstock at them, yelling, "Say howdy to my Whig constituents fer me when you see 'em! Tell 'em I'm still here in Tex—"

Sergeant Nuñez darted in under the swinging rifle and struck with his sword and twenty Mexican bayonets flashed forward.

It didn't matter whom Tack hit now. He aimed his shotgun straight down and pumped both barrels into the yelling soldiers below. But it was impossible to stem the flooding tide of Mexicans pouring into the Alamo. Tack looked across to the church roof. Dickinson and Bonham were

180

still on the ramp working one of the 12-pounders, spraying the chapel yard with nails, musket balls, links of chain and scrap iron.

"Bonham!" Tack shouted. "Look out!" He pointed toward the compound, where Morales' men had swung around the 18-pounder.

Bonham, tall, thin, powder-blackened, looked and raised a hand to Tack, a sort of salute. Then he and Dickinson blew another load of iron trash into the yard.

The 18-pounder slammed into the church, tearing the air alive with grape. Dickinson went down, so did Bonham. The Mexicans swarmed into the rubble-choked nave and smoke-swirling rooms and went at the civilians with bullets and bayonets, killing the men and young teen-age boys. They spared the women and little children. They heaved one man—Jacob Walker from Nacogdoches—out of the sacristy on the point of their bayonets, just like a bale of hay.

Tack stepped back and let out his breath. He walked across the lonely roof and looked down at the long barracks. Bullets went *whock whock* against the parapet. He reloaded the shotgun. They would be coming for him in a minute—across the roof of the barracks. He knew that.

The act of dying, he now realized, was nothing. It was quick and sharp—a brilliant blinding final flash. It was having to give up life, the act of living, that was painful.

Living was a tall steamboat standing down the river, with your hands on the worn wheel spokes and old Ben yanking the whistle cord beside you and the wheezy ear-splintering notes echoing down, down, down the bayous. Living was cantering across the prairies in the morning with old Tom riding at your side and with the purple sage in bloom for acres and acres around and the wild turkeys gobble-gobbling in the sand and a rabbit going away all driving hind paws and powder-puff tail. Living was Nap grinning at you for no reason at all and Hank putting his hand on your shoulder and saying "Luck, Tack."

But he wasn't sorry for any of it. The fight they had fought here had been a good fight and he told himself that he would rather die young and fast and with a purpose than old and sick in a rumpled bed for no purpose at all.

If we could hold them up here, he thought, *then we can hold them everywhere. Then we can stop them, turn them back, and then we will have won.* That was good. That was far better than the chance most men ever had to do something with meaning. Something that was truly valid. Yes. He would buy that.

Well—it really did matter after all, didn't it?

They were coming now—a dozen, two dozen of them; coming across the artillery quarters roof, and now the long barracks roof, past Richardson Perry and the three Mexican sergeants and the two dead lieutenants; coming with muskets and bayonets and three scaling ladders. Tack raised the shotgun and opened fire.

In the last quick, brilliant flash of living—with the ladder tops crashing against the parapet and the glittering dazzle of dawn-struck bayonets lancing upward and with the phosphorescent-like musket explosions—Tack felt that he was plunging into a dizzying and golden flutter of stalks of wheat. And it was beautiful, like sinking into a deep coruscating web of shining glory. Then . . .

WARNELL

I am alive.

Doesn't seem possible, yet it's true. I try to move and an ice pick of pain stabs under my right armpit. That's right. I remember now. That Mex sergeant got me with his sword. Then I fell backwards and part of the palisade came down on me and I passed out.

I try to raise my head. Can't. Something on top of it. It's that section of toppled palisade. It's leaning against the little earth embankment and I'm wedged under the hollow angle. Good place to be, I guess. Maybe the Mexicans won't find me in here.

Good. Here's a narrow slot between the pales and the dirt . . . I can look out . . . see the chapel yard and a little of the Plaza. There's Crockett's coonskin cap lying over there in the dirt, still glaring defiance like a masked bandit. There's General Castrillón, Colonel Almonte, and Captain Urizza (think that's his name) moving among the ruins, inspecting the dead.

The Mexicans have just found six survivors in the low barracks and are bringing them out. All six have surrendered but I don't think it will do them much good. However, who can blame them for trying or hoping? What can six unarmed men accomplish against two thousand soldiers? General Castrillón is keeping his troops away from them. Rather a kindly *caballero*, I imagine. Evidently he doesn't want them to be massacred. Can't make out who the six are from here. . . .

Uh-uh, here comes the great man himself. Santa Anna.

"It was but a small affair, after all," he says to Captain Urizza with a depreciatory wave of his hand. "It took but an hour and a half to annihilate the stupid Texans."

"*Si, El Presidente*," Urizza says, "but there were only 183 of them. And there were over 1,800 of us in the attack."

"It means nothing," Santa Anna says grandly. "The important thing is that we have removed this thorn in our side. What are our casualties?"

"One thousand, we believe, Excellency."

"*One thousand!* Goliath's foster father and stepbrother! Did you say ONE THOUSAND, *hombre?*"

"*Si*," Urizza says meekly.

There are two officers standing right in front of my hide hole. They look pretty glum about the whole affair. One of them says, "Another smashing victory like this will be the ruin of us!"

Santa Anna does not look quite so pleased with himself now. He looks a little sick. Here comes General Castrillón.

"Sir, I have taken six prisoners alive. What shall I do—"

Santa Anna cries, "How many times have I told you I take no prisoners? Kill them immediately!"

The general's own staff have sprung forward to get their share of blood out of this day's dirty work. Brave officers! Oh yes—when it comes to cutting down unarmed prisoners with their swords.

There! Idiots! In their impetuousness they have almost killed General Castrillón himself! Santa Anna is having a hopping fit. Hope he pops a blood vessel!

The Mexicans are herding the women and children from the church now. There are about a dozen of them. All

Mexicans except for Mrs. Dickinson and her little daughter. Santa Anna is being very courteous to them, offering them blankets and food and water, telling them that they are free to go.

What's this? A Mexican civilian is coming from the church under an armed escort. It is Brigido Guerrero, one of our Mexican volunteers. He must have been hiding in there among the women.

"*Compadres!*" Guerrero cries. "Listen to me! I am but a poor victim of circumstance. *Amigos,* I swear to you I was not on the side of the Texans. They made me stay in the Alamo! They kept me a prisoner! What could I do against such evil men?"

Heyday! He's actually talking them out of killing him! Well, it looks as if there will be at least one survivor after all . . . unless I can get away. . . .

The Mexicans have already started a victory celebration. Nice men, very nice. A couple of them have just killed a poor old tomcat claiming that it deserved to die because it was an *Americano.*

Lord—give me strength to get out of this. Strength enough to come back and fight them again. That's not much to ask, is it?

They've just found Joe.

A couple of them are bringing him over to Santa Anna. He looks gray with fright, and who can blame him? Someone has nicked his left arm with a bayonet, I guess. Anyway, it's bleeding.

"You have nothing to fear from me," Santa Anna assures him. "We are not making this war against your race. You are free to go."

Joe bobs his head and edges out of the circle of officers. He's coming this way. . . .

Joe . . . Joe, you are climbing now right over my head . . . the pales just above my back give with your weight and you don't even know I'm here below you. Take me with

186

you, Joe. Help me out of this. If I could only call out to you for help, as you once called to me. Ah, Joe . . . now you're going . . . gone . . . and I'm left behind.

All right. I knew from the moment I came to that I would have to get myself out of this mess. Alone and unaided and wounded. If this filthy wound just won't start bleeding again. If it just won't hemorrhage . . . if I can hold out till dark . . . yes, while they celebrate themselves silly. In the dark I'll escape. Good. That's settled then.

If I don't pass out. Please, Lord; I don't pass out. All right? Let me hold together until it is dark and then I'll make a try for the river. Because it's important, you see? Important that I get away. Not me—Henry Warnell as an individual—but just one defender of the Alamo as a spirit of the Alamo, to spread the word, the alarm, to tell them, all of them, how we fought and died here.

Because they must all realize what they are up against: insidious butchers, aye, but little craven, frightened men, too, like their leader. . . .

He is having the bodies of the Texans cremated now, stacking them like cordwood in the Plaza. He holds out the corpses of Travis and Bowie and Crockett because he wants positive identification from Mrs. Dickinson and the other civilian survivors.

Even in death he is still afraid of them. Afraid they aren't really dead. Afraid they will rise again and take another stand against him.

Poor fool! He might as well identify all of them. Because we are all a threat to him. Death has not changed that. We will all live on in memory: Allen and Brown and Hendricks and Perry and Mitchell and Tackett . . .

Tack. Where is he now? What has become of him? Is his body in that mass cremation? I got him into this, and now (with luck) I must leave him here. And I don't know if he ever really knew what he was doing here, if he understood exactly what it was he was dying for.

I hope he did. I hope at the very last he understood everything.

Because it is important that they all understand. All Americans, all free men everywhere. Important that they remember the Alamo forever.

Dark now. The Mexicans still whooping it up in the Plaza.

All right. Here we go. All of us. All 183 together.

It looks good. Think I'm going to make it—I mean we. *We* are going to make it.

The beautiful dark, battle-trampled weeds are right ahead, now, and . . .

AUTHOR'S NOTE

Except for the following characters—Ben Burrows, Toff Beeker, Captain Pennypacker, Amos Rynd, Guy Perrez, Sheriff Poole and Lieutenant Tampas, everyone named in this narrative played an actual part in the Texas Insurrection of 1835–36.

It should be understood that when writing about a group of relatively unknown people who died abruptly over 125 years ago, a certain amount of guesswork must be employed in the reconstruction of their lives. Some liberties had to be taken in order to build a fictional-fact story around these people.

For instance, Louis Rose came to Texas in 1828, not in 1835. However, he *was* a professional soldier from the Napoleonic wars, and he *was* the only Texan who refused to cross "Travis' line."

Absolutely nothing is known about Napoleon "Nap" Mitchell except the manner in which he died, which Mrs. Alsbury witnessed.

Nothing is known about Richard Allen, Richardson Perry, Robert Brown or Tom Hendricks, except that they died in the Alamo on that fateful dawn of March 6, 1836.

James M. Rose, who figured in the burning of La Villita, should not be confused with Louis Rose. They were not related. James Rose was in fact the nephew of ex-President Madison.

189

West Point training or not, Colonel Fannin surrendered to General Urrea on March 19 without much of a fight. One week later Fannin and his entire force (400 Texans) were executed by the Mexicans.

Travis, Bowie and Crockett were three of Texas' greatest heroes; yet it must be remembered that they were also mortal men, given to mortal faults. But their all-too-human shortcomings are not important. What really matters is that these three men gave Texas and America a heritage, a tradition, a sense of national pride that will endure just as long as one American can communicate with another American.

Exactly how many Mexicans fell at the Alamo will never be known. Estimates range from 600 to 1,600. Estimates on the Texans usually vary between 180 and 187. But those who claim 187 forget that Louis Rose deserted, and that John Smith and James L. Allen rode out as the last messengers. Smith went on March 3, Allen on March 5. James Allen was sixteen years old. He later became Mayor of Indianola.

As with Custer's Last Stand, the Battle of the Alamo has always been shrouded with rumors, folklore and legend, until the actual truth has become all but obscured. Let us consider the most interesting legends:

Legend: Travis drew the line with his sword.

Maybe, maybe not. Many historians now doubt it. Still and all, it *sounds* like the sort of thing Travis would do. Remember, Travis was more dramatic than, say, any of our most modern "method actors"—with far more reason to be dramatic. Let it stand. I think he drew the line.

Legend: Davy Crockett surrendered to the Mexicans.

I doubt it. First, because it doesn't sound like Crockett. Second, because the facts don't coincide. The six men who surrendered came from the low barracks in the Plaza, and they were executed on the spot. But Mrs. Dickinson said that the first thing she saw when she came from the church was Crockett's body. So—if she saw his body in the chapel yard, and if the six who surrendered were killed in the Plaza, how did Crockett's body span the distance between the two points, and why? And third, Sergeant Felix Nuñez (from whom we learn of the Tennessean who fought alone with his back to the corral wall) implies that this lone American woodsman was indeed the mighty Crockett.

Let us bury Davy Crockett once and for all in this honorable memory: his long rifle in his hands, his back to a wall, defiantly facing a ring of enemies.

Legend: Davy Crockett was the last to fall.

Conflicting Legend: Jim Bowie was the last to fall.

I doubt both romantic tales, for these reasons: Bowie was in the low barracks and that position fell right after the Plaza and the long barracks were taken. Thus Bowie must have been killed when Morales' men swarmed into the low barracks.

Now for Crockett. If (as Mrs. Dickinson claims) Crockett fell in the chapel yard, then he would have had to have fallen before Morales fired on the church with the 18-pounder; which means that Bonham and Dickinson (both fighting on the church ramp) fell after him.

It is my contention that the last man to fall was Robert Evans from New York—who was already inside the church when the Mexicans stormed it, and who, wounded, tried to crawl to the powder room to blow up the magazine with a torch. A Mexican bullet killed him.

Legend: There was a lone survivor.

Very possible. I discount Louis Rose who escaped before the battle, and I have my doubts about Brigido Guerrero because there is no proof that he was actually a combative defender of the Alamo. But there is evidence that Henry Warnell managed to escape from the Alamo after the assault. He made his way to Port Lavacca, where he died three months later from his wound. This, at best, is only a possibility—yet I like to believe that Hank made it.

Now for a hardbound historic fact: on April 21, 1836,

General Sam Houston whipped General Santa Anna as no general had ever before been whipped. In an 18-minute battle at San Jacinto the Texans killed 630 Mexicans, wounded 200, and took 730 prisoners. Santa Anna was among the prisoners. The Texans suffered 9 killed and 34 wounded, out of an army of 783 men.

The Texas battle cry at San Jacinto was, "Remember the Alamo!"

And Tack? He is a composite of all the young American volunteers who fought and died in the Alamo, with their moments of self-doubt and fear and regret, and yet who—in their last furious and glorious moment—realized they were dying for a cause that would remain deathless forever.

ROBERT EDMOND ALTER

The Author

This is the seventh novel Robert Edmond Alter has written for young people all of which have been published by Putnam.

When he left home at the age of sixteen, Bob Alter was determined that he would make social work his career. At twenty, after working as a citrus picker and at a score of other jobs which included being a movie extra, he found himself in the army. By the time he had reached his early thirties, he was back to an ambition he held even before his fascination with social work; he would be a writer.

In addition to his juvenile novels, Alter has also published one adult novel, and has been a frequent contributor to the *Saturday Evening Post, Alfred Hitchcock's Mystery Magazine, Argosy*, and *Boys' Life*. Bob Alter lives in Altadena, California, with his wife and teen-age daughter.